Tanner

The Splintered Hearts Series

Nicola Jane

Copyright © 2019 – Original Edition by Nicola Jane

Copyright © 2022 – Second Edition by Nicola Jane

All rights reserved.

No portion of this book may be reproduced in any form without written permission from the publisher or author, except as permitted by U.K. copyright law.

Meet The Team

Cover design: Francessca Wingfield - Wingfield Designs
Editor: Rebecca Vazquez - Dark Syde Books
Formatting: Nicola Miller

Disclaimer:
This book is a work of fiction. The names, characters, places, and incidents are all products of the author's imagination and are not to be construed as real. Any similarities are entirely coincidental.

Spelling:
Please note, this author resides in the United Kingdom and is using British English. Therefore,

some words may be viewed as incorrect or spelled incorrectly. However, they are not.

Acknowledgments

For my readers, who hate Cooper, Kain and Tanner, but also love them just as much.

Contents

A note from the Author	IX
Playlist	X
PROLOGUE	1
CHAPTER ONE	4
CHAPTER TWO	21
CHAPTER THREE	35
CHAPTER FOUR	48
CHAPTER FIVE	62
CHAPTER SIX	77
CHAPTER SEVEN	91
CHAPTER EIGHT	105
CHAPTER NINE	123
CHAPTER TEN	136
CHAPTER ELEVEN	152
CHAPTER TWELVE	167
CHAPTER THIRTEEN	185

CHAPTER FOURTEEN	195
Six months later . . .	205
1. A note from me to you	207
2. Popular books by Nicola Jane	209

A note from the Author

This book deals with cheating that has already happened in the relationship. It focusses on life after cheating and how we move forward, or in some cases, back. There is also some discussions about childhood sexual abuse, although the author does not go into detail.

Playlist

I Don't Wanna Know – Dylan Matthew
I Hate U, I Love You – Gnash ft. Olivia O'Brien
Let Her Go – Passenger
You Broke Me First – Tate McRae
Bruises – Lewis Capaldi
All I Want – Kodaline
Lose You To Love You – Selena Gomez
Let Me Down Slowly – Alec Benjamin
It Will Rain – Bruno Mars
Same Old Love – Selena Gomez
Wicked Game – Grace Carter
Now You're Gone – Tom Walker ft. Zara Larsson
Confessions – Usher
Part of Me – Katy Perry
River of Tears – Alessia Cara

Shout Out to my Ex – Little Mix
New Rules – Dua Lipa
What Now – Rhianna
One Life – Ed Sheeran
Pointless – Lewis Capaldi

You can listen, here:

https://open.spotify.com/user/omqkvqsa4uybu79Oss5iluvly?si=ON1gx-sopQDSuRWuBd8BA6g&utm_source=copy-link

PROLOGUE

9 years earlier...
Brook

"We're too young, Brook, what the hell?" Tanner stares down at the two white sticks I'd produced just minutes ago. I knew he'd take the news badly. After all, we haven't been together very long. I watch with tears in my eyes as he paces back and forth. He's completely naked, but for once, it doesn't distract me. I pull the sheets around me tighter and remain quiet. I'm scared. I hadn't been expecting it, and I'd only done the tests to shut my friend up after I told her my period was four days late. "I'll call the club doctor now and get it sorted."

"What do you mean?" I ask.

"I mean, we get rid of it. I can't share you yet, Brook. I haven't had enough time with you."

Tanner is intense, so intense that sometimes I wonder what I've gotten myself into. He'd bugged me relentlessly for a date after spotting me in the street one day, and since then, he's hardly left my side. Sometimes, I catch him just staring at me. Friends think it's weird, but after years of growing up in foster care, it's nice to have someone who likes me so much, they don't want to be apart from me.

"Shouldn't we discuss it a bit more?" I ask. I feel the least we owe this poor unborn child, that we'd made together, is a discussion.

"Brook, we aren't ready for a baby. You're seventeen, for starters, and what hope does a kid have with me raising it? My dad's a drunk, and he blames that on having me so young."

"You're not a drunk," I muttered.

"Look at your parents. You've spent most of your life in foster care. We can't look after a kid."

I sigh, thinking maybe he's right. We don't have the best track record for parents. Tanner pushes me back onto the bed and lays over me, placing a kiss on my lips. "Trust me, baby, the time's not right. I'm not saying it'll never happen . . . I'm just saying not now, okay?"

I nod, letting him run kisses along my jaw and down my neck. "Let me get established in the club, get some cash behind us so I can buy us a home, and then we can get married. I have a whole future planned for us, and babies don't happen yet."

CHAPTER ONE

Present day
　Tanner

"Tanner, I need you on this, where the fuck are you?" demands Cooper, my club President. "I'm sick of having to track you down. You don't answer my calls. You don't check in. What use is an Enforcer if he's never around?"

I sigh. He's grating on me with his nagging wife rants. Of course, I'm off radar, cos I just lost the love of my life and the last thing I wanna do is collect debts for the club. Movement from the apartment catches my eye. "Look, Pres, can I call you back? I'm in the middle of something," I say in a quiet voice.

"No, Tanner, you can't fucking call me back. Get your arse back to the club. We need a chat." He disconnects the call, and I shove the mobile back in my pocket. Fuck Cooper. He might be my Pres, but he needs to give me a break and see the shit I've got going on right now. The door to her place opens and I step back into the shadows. The last thing I need is her to call the Polices on me again.

"I swear you do it on purpose," her voice rings out into the empty street. She's smiling. I miss that smile. Brook, my ex, my world. She looks amazing in her tight-fit denim jeans, low cut white shirt, and leather jacket. She wears her hair different these days. It's longer and shapes her face better.

"I do not. It was a last-minute decision. James was feeling low, and I thought to myself, what's the best way to cheer him up? You could have said no," replies Henry Edge, owner of Edgy Cuts Hair Salon. Gay, single, and thirty years old, Henry is Brook's new boss and, from the amount of time they spend together, I'd say new best friend.

"Me, turn down a night out, erm, as if." She laughs again, and my heart aches. I want to make her laugh like that again. I'd give anything.

I follow them, staying back in the shadows until they reach their destination—a small wine bar just around the corner from Brook's new place.

My mobile vibrates in my pocket, but I wait for them to go inside the bar before answering. "You'd better be on your way, Tanner," comes Cooper's pissed-off voice for a second time.

"I told you, I'm busy right now. I'll be there as soon as I can."

"Are you watching her again?" he presses. I keep quiet, not wanting to lie to my President but not wanting to reveal the truth either. "You know what, don't even answer that because it'll make me want to kick your arse even more. Melissa has turned up here looking for you, and unless you want my ol' lady to start hunting you down, I suggest you get back here. The ol' ladies are already staring Melissa down. It's like a damn witch hunt, and I don't wanna be the referee in your clusterfuck."

"Cooper, can't you have a word with them? I can't be there just yet." Melissa can handle her own. She won't be upset by the ol' ladies being bitchy, but she won't be happy having to wait around for me, especially as I'd been avoiding her calls all week. I need to make sure Brook gets home safe before I even think of leaving.

"No, I can't! Get back here or I'll tell Melissa exactly where you are and what you've been doing, and then I'll tell Mila that you're still stalking one of her best friends."

"Great, thanks for nothing, Pres." I disconnect the call, in temper. I get a glimpse of Brook through the bar window. Since starting her new job, she's made new friends, pushing the Hammers MC firmly out of her life. Most of the ol' ladies hold me responsible for that, and I don't blame them. It's totally my fault. I got drunk and cheated on Brook with Melissa, a nineteen-year-old club whore, and then to add insult to injury, Melissa turned up a few months later announcing that she was pregnant. Brook wants a child so desperately, but she's been told by doctors that she can't conceive naturally.

So, now, here we are. She's moved on. Left me, left the club, and started a new life, one that doesn't involve any of us.

By the time I reach the club, Cooper is waiting outside with Melissa. Her hands rest on her small bump, and the sight repulses me. I hate myself for what I've done, and that bump is a constant reminder.

I park up and make my way over, fist bumping Cooper in greeting before turning to Melissa. "Hey," I mutter, keeping my eyes lowered.

"Shit, Tanner, you can look at me, yah know. I ain't that disgusting," she snaps.

"What're you doing here?" I ask.

"I need money. I've tried calling you, but you never answer. What if something happens to the kid and I need you?" she demands. I want to tell her that I wouldn't care, which makes me an arse, but it's how I feel. "I even messaged Brook on social media, and the cheeky cow deleted it and then blocked my profile."

"You contacted Brook?" It immediately annoys me. The last thing Brook needs is Melissa contacting her to track me down. "Don't do that again." I pull my wallet out and take out a bunch of twenties, stuffing them in her waiting hand. "What do you need it for?"

"Baby stuff, obviously." She rolls her eyes and then marches away, flicking her hair over her shoulder as she goes. I stand beside Cooper in silence, watching as a black car slows outside the gates. Melissa gets inside and it drives away at speed.

"Aren't you worried about who she's with, what she spends the money on?" asks Cooper.

"Nope." I head inside, where a few of my brothers are playing a game of cards in the bar. Cash is piled in the middle, something I'd usually take part in, but right now, I need to shower and get back to Brook.

Mila steps in front of me, her expression hard. Since becoming Cooper's ol' lady, she's really toughened up, keeping us guys in order. "Not now, Mila. I don't have time."

I know instantly it's the wrong thing to say because her hands go to her hips and her eyes narrow. She isn't budging out of my way until she's said what she needs to, and so I drop down onto the nearest stool and sit back, waiting for the lecture to begin.

"Sit up straight," she snaps. I do it, mainly because it'll just make her speech longer if I don't. "Brook knows you're still following her. She moved to a new place to stop this bullshit and then you turn up there. It has to stop, Tanner."

"I'm making sure she's okay," I mutter feebly.

"She doesn't need you to. She's moving on."

"What does that mean?" I sit up farther, suddenly interested in the conversation.

"It means you need to stop following her. It's weird now you're not together. I mean, it was weird before but . . . well, now, it's stalkerish."

"Has she met someone else?" It'll kill me, but I need to know.

Mila doesn't meet my eyes. Instead, she knots her fingers, a sure sign she's uncomfortable. "Not yet, but she's talking about it. It's been three months now, and it's time she got back out there."

"Three months is fuck all. She loves me, she'll never be able to move on from that!" I'm angry, and my raised voice gets the attention of some of the guys. Kain, the club's VP, stands and slowly makes his way over.

"It doesn't matter if she loves you. She will never be with you now, and so getting back out there will help her move forward. Stay away from her, Tanner."

"Things good, brother?" asks Kain casually. I don't have the energy to answer. Instead, I take myself off to my room. I'll shower and get back to Brook. We need to talk.

Brook

Henry revels in matchmaking. He said it's where his expertise truly lies. So, the fact he's now chatting to the gorgeous six-foot, dark-haired man I'd glanced at ten minutes ago doesn't surprise me. Occasionally, they both look my way, and I know my face is crimson with embarrassment.

James places a tray of empty glasses down on the table and the bartender follows, adding two bottles of Champagne. It's how these guys roll. I'm a little less extravagant, coming from a poorer background. I appreciate money, and even if I could afford the ridiculously overpriced Champagne, I wouldn't buy it.

James pours me a glass, sliding it towards me. "I'll get my drink, James. You know I don't drink that stuff."

"Tonight, you can entertain my overindulgence because I'm sad and I get to boss everyone around."

I laugh, taking the glass. "Emotional blackmail is pathetic."

James is Henry's best friend. Both are gay and proud—sometimes it feels like a competition between the pair to see who's the proudest.

Henry owns a hair salon called Edgy Cuts. He opened it five years ago, and James was his very first employee. Then came William, straight and handsome. I'm sure women came to Edgy purely to have his fingers running through their hair. He's mega talented and has won awards for his styling abilities. After Will came Blake. She's ridiculously girly and, standing at five-foot-three and of slim build, she certainly ticks a lot of men's boxes. I joined the team just two months ago, and so far, I'm loving it. Everyone welcomed me, and instantly I felt like one of the family.

It'd been a few years since I've worked, because at sixteen I'd met my ex, Tanner, and he'd convinced me to finish the course I'd begun as a trainee stylist. He said I wouldn't need to work because he wanted to look after me. I was in love, and I was happy, as long as he was, so I cut hair at the MC clubhouse, which he's a member of, for the guys and their ol' ladies, but I didn't bother to chase my dream.

"Earth to Brook," says James, waving his hand in front of my face. "Male incoming."

I look over to where the handsome stranger is following Henry to our table and my face immediately flushes again. It's also been a long time since I spoke to men other than the bikers at the Hammers MC.

"Brook, this is Anton. He's thirty-two and works in a bank."

"Oh." I smile, unsure of how to respond. The guys are always pushing me to date, but I'm far too inexperienced in that scene. Plus, it's only been three months since Tanner and I broke up, we were together a long time and I'm still not sure how to function without him.

"And you work in a salon?" asks Anton, taking a seat. I nod, sipping nervously on my Champagne.

"Brook." The sound of that familiar voice causes me to spill Champagne down my chin. I swipe at it, using the back of my hand, and look up at Tanner, who towers over the table, gaining everyone's full attention.

"What are you doing here?" My voice wobbles with nerves. It's been months since I've spoken to him, but I've felt him watching me from a distance. It's like an invisible connection we have, although lately, I've not felt him and so I'm surprised to find him here, staring at me with those eyes so full of guilt and shame.

"We need to talk." He shifts awkwardly, keeping his head lowered and his hands stuffed into his pockets.

"Now's not a good time." I don't have the strength to speak with Tanner. My heart still hurts after what he's done to me.

"Now is perfect. Get up." I hear James suck in a wistful breath. I know how Tanner affects women with his muscles, his dark beard, and his tattoos, looking like the ultimate bad boy-come-Hercules, and I'm not surprised he has the same effect on my gay friend.

"Tanner, not now," I say a little more firmly. Tanner doesn't know how to deal with me when I refuse him. Months ago, when we were still in a relationship, he'd chase me around and fuck me into submission. Now it isn't an option, I can see he isn't sure how to handle the situation. It's another reminder of how we never communicated outside the bedroom.

Without another word, he turns and leaves. I can feel everyone's shocked eyes on me, but I focus on my drink, knocking back the bubbly liquid and wincing at the bitter aftertaste.

"That was Tanner?" Blake eventually squeaks. I nod, smiling when James tops up my empty glass. "Oh my god, he's hot. Why didn't you say how hot he is?"

"How are you still sitting there like nothing's happened. I'd have jumped on his retreating back and wrestled him to the ground, then stripped him and ran my tongue all over those rock-hard pecs of his," growls Henry, and I laugh. Months ago, that's probably what I would have wanted to do, but these days, I'm much more restrained because I know how much power he has to destroy me.

"Anton, how long have you been in banking?" I ask brightly. A change in topic is exactly what's needed.

Despite Henry's many attempts to get me drunk, I stopped drinking after two glasses of Champagne. Seeing Tanner changed my mood, and once everyone in the group had gotten up to dance, I'd made my excuses and left.

Anton insisted on walking me home, which I insisted was completely unnecessary, but he was so pushy about it, I gave in, and now, I have my rape alarm gripped tightly in my jacket pocket, just in case.

"I'd love to see you again, Brook," he says as we slow right outside my apartment block.

"Yeah, maybe." Things feel awkward and forced, but I take the business card he holds out for me. *Is this how people do things these days, by handing out business cards?*

"Give me a call and maybe we can arrange lunch one day next week?"

I nod, shoving the little card into my pocket. "Thanks for walking me home. Goodnight." I don't miss the disappointment on his face right before I walk up the steps, but I'm not going to kiss the guy or invite him inside. I'm a fourth date minimum kind of girl, at least, I think I am.

I use my security fob to get in, and I'm startled to see Tanner sitting on the floor of the lobby, waiting by the lift. "Tanner, what are you doing here?" I ask, sighing. My heart rate doubles, thudding hard in my chest.

"Did you kiss him? I couldn't bear to watch that, but now I need to know."

"You've been watching me again? You have to stop. Go home or I'm calling Cooper to come get you."

"Did you kiss him?" he growls, his eyes burning into my own. They're full of pain and a part of me is glad. He deserves to hurt after everything he's done. I loved him so much, and I still do. We were inseparable and intense, and we knew each other inside out. I could sense him in a crowd, we were that close. He couldn't bear to be away from me, and I guess I felt the same, which made his cheating even more painful.

"That's none of your business, Tanner. Get the fuck out." I pull out my mobile phone and hold it up in warning. I'm not afraid to rat him out to his Pres if he doesn't leave.

Tanner pushes to his feet and stuffs his hands back into his pockets. "Please, Brook. I'll beg if you want me to. Five minutes . . . just five." He's tugging on my heart strings with that lost boy look on his chiselled face. I roll my eyes in defeat and press the button for the lift.

Tanner steps in first, standing behind me. The pull between us as the doors slide closed is so intense, I squeeze my eyes shut and pray for it to move faster so I can escape the proximity. It doesn't feel right being so close and not being wrapped in his arms.

Stepping out into the passage, I turn right and unlock my apartment door. I step to one side and let Tanner go in ahead of me. He stops beside me, almost pushing against me yet not quite touching. His hands are still firmly stuffed into his pockets, and I wonder if he feels the urge to touch me too. I watch as he closes his eyes and tilts his head closer before inhaling. "You changed your shampoo," he whispers, disappointment in his tone. "You smell different."

"Your five minutes have started, Tanner," I say, keeping my voice steady. The truth is, I miss his scent too, the mix of whisky, spicy cologne, and leather. I changed mine on purpose, because he used to tell me he'd bottle it if he could, that it calmed his soul. I wanted to reinvent myself to be far from anything he could use to his advantage.

Once inside, I turn on the coffee machine and it springs to life. I set up one cup, not wanting to make him comfortable. "So," I push, "you wanted to talk."

"Are you okay?" he begins.

"You came here to ask how I am?" I scoff, glaring at him. Laughing, I shake my head in disappointment. "How do you think I am, Tanner?" It's a stupid question and it pisses me off.

"You seem okay. New job, nice apartment, new clothes, different hair, new friends, different scent." He reels off the list and then shrugs his shoulders in a sulky manner.

"Did you want to see me sitting in a corner, rocking and crying?"

"Of course not, I just . . ." He trails off.

"Because I do that too, Tanner. None of this has been easy for me." I sigh angrily. "How's Melissa?" I ask coldly. I don't give a shit about her, and he knows it, but I want to see his reaction. I'd instructed Mila and Harper not to tell me about anything club-related, especially not anything about Tanner and Melissa, but I can't help being curious. Is he in a relationship with her? Do they have a nursery set up for the baby? Do they share our old bedroom at the clubhouse? The questions run through my head, and I stir my coffee to distract myself.

"I don't want to talk about her. It isn't why I came here. We have a follow-up appointment with your gynaecologist. Did you remember?"

I laugh, hardly believing he'd dare to bring that up. We made that appointment before we split up to discuss different avenues for us to have a baby since I'd been told I can't conceive. Tanner was dead set against the idea of other avenues, but I think he agreed because he felt sorry for me. He knew I wanted kids, and when I found out that wasn't possible, it broke my heart. The truth was, Tanner didn't want to share me with anyone, not even his own baby.

"Joint appointments ended when we did, Tanner," I snap. "Your time is up, leave."

Tanner takes a mug from the dishwasher and places it on the side. He pours himself a black coffee, ignoring my request for him to go. "I think we should still go. It took us a long time to get the appointment. He was booked up for months in advance."

"Are you kidding me right now?" I snap in disbelief. "We broke up, so I don't need to talk about having a kid with you because it's impossible."

"It's not impossible," he mutters, staring into his mug. "Maybe I can still give you that."

I suck in a breath, then my chest begins to hurt again and I rub it, trying to make it stop. "What the hell are you talking about?"

"I know how badly you want a baby. I can still give you that. The doctors can do so much these days, test tube babies or planting the egg straight into your womb. I looked it up on the internet. I'll pay for whatever they can do to give you a baby."

"Oh my god, you need to leave," I mutter, shaking my head in disbelief.

"Why is it such a bad idea, Brook? You can have the baby you always wanted."

"And have you in my life forever, I don't think so."

"Is that so bad?"

"Yes, it's bad. I don't want you around as a constant reminder of how much you've hurt me, Tanner. I wanted a baby with you for so long, and you always told me it wasn't the right time. Did you have that same conversation with Melissa? Did you discuss timing and your financial situation not being stable enough?" I'm ranting, but I can't stop myself, I've bottled so much up since our split. "When we found out I couldn't have kids, my first thought was that it was your fault. Did you know that?" Tanner shakes his head, hurt clear on his face. "If I hadn't aborted our first baby because you weren't ready, then I'd be a mum now. I feel like God took away my chance because I screwed up the first miracle he gave me."

"That's not fair, Brook. You weren't ready either."

"I was ready, but I was scared I'd lose you. I was pathetic and weak, and I thought I needed you to survive. How dare you come here and offer me a baby after what you've done to me! Your life will be spent worrying about Melissa taking care of your child, because I can tell you now, she will not be a good mother. She doesn't want your baby. She doesn't want to be a mum. You picked the worst person to raise your child, and now, you have to live with that."

"This isn't you. You sound bitter and hateful and that's not the Brook I once knew. All this," he snaps, tugging at my new leather jacket, "this trendy shit you wear, it isn't you. My Brook liked summer dresses and Doc Martens boots. She loved staying home and watching movies, not going out partying every night with stuck-up bastards who drink Champagne like water. It's all fake, and you're being fake. You hardly see anyone from the club, now you prefer the company of your new work friends!" He's shouting, his face red with anger, but his tone mocking.

"Maybe this was the Brook I should have been. If I'd have been this Brook, then you wouldn't have given me a second look and my heart wouldn't hurt so much right now." I place my coffee down and head for the bathroom, locking the door behind me. I pull out my phone and dial Cooper's number.

CHAPTER TWO

Tanner

I wait patiently but she doesn't return. I feel like a dick, and so I head after her. If I don't make this right, she'll never speak to me again. Her apartment is small but cosy. She's decorated it in girly shit like flowery pictures and sparkly lamps but there're no pictures on the walls, or photographs. Brook always loved photographs. I tap on the locked bathroom door.

"Baby, please come out and talk to me. I'm sorry, I shouldn't have said any of that." She ignores me, and I slide down the wall, my arse hitting the fluffy carpet. "You're wrong. I would've still looked your way. The denim suits you, and I like your new hair. Truth is, you could've been wearing a paper bag and I'd have still found you and made you mine. Since you left, Brook, I've hardly slept. I feel like I can't breathe right, and my head's a mess. Being near you calms it all and I stop all the crazy shit, and there's been a lot of that since you went. I've been fucking it all up."

Pools of blood flash through my mind. I've gone back to cage fighting to try and tame the beast inside me, the one that wants to take Brook and lock her away. Without the fighting, I'd have killed that suited piece of crap who walked my Brook home tonight. But I can't tell her about the fighting, she'd be disappointed, and I'd hate for her to be anymore disappointed in me.

The buzzer to Brook's intercom rings out. "You'd better go and answer that. It's for you," she says from behind the door.

I groan aloud. "You called him? Jesus Christ, Brook, I only want to talk." She doesn't bother to answer, so I get to my feet and press the intercom to my ear. "Yeah?"

"Get out here or I'm coming in to get you. I have five guys with me." Cooper sounds pissed. I hang up and go back to the bathroom door.

"Okay, you win. I'll go, but consider my offer, Brook."

Cooper wasn't kidding. Outside of Brook's apartment, five motorcycles are lined up alongside mine. "A little over the top, don't yah think?" I ask, raising an eyebrow.

"Not really," snaps Cooper. "We never know which Tanner we're gonna be faced with these days."

"Well, tonight, I'm the frustrated one, so I'm off to see Frank about a fight," I mutter, swinging my leg over my motorcycle.

"Great. I'd like to watch you get your arse beat. See you there."

I roll my eyes and push on my helmet. I never get beat, and he knows it, the dick.

We arrive at the warehouse situated on some London back street. It's busy, and Frank, the organiser, is surrounded by people all waving cash in his face while he takes down the next lot of bets. I'm down to fight the winner of the current fight, and both guys in the cage are good. I make my way to the corner of the room and change. Cooper watches, loitering, which usually means he's got something to say. "Spit it out, Pres," I mutter, stretching out my arms and then throwing a few air punches to warm up.

"I don't wanna sound like a pussy, man, but I'm worried about you."

"You failed. You totally sound like a pussy," I mutter, moving my head from side to side to loosen the muscles.

"Seriously, Tanner, you've always been a crazy motherfucker, but all this stalking is weird. Mila thinks Brook might call the Police and file an official report if you don't quit."

"If it was Mila, would you walk away and move on?"

"That's different, I have kids with her. This isn't healthy. I know you love her, Tann, we all do, and the place ain't the same without that crazy little fairy around, but maybe it's time you let her go. It's what she wants, man."

I curl my fists tight. If Cooper was in my shoes, he'd behave the exact same, kids or not, and so would Kain. Those guys are just as crazy about their women. "I can't breathe without her, Pres. You know how that feels, right? And I can't just walk away like she's nothing. I hate not knowing where she is and who's she's with. It's torture. And I deserve it, I know that, but have my back on this, cos I ain't giving up on her."

Cooper thinks over my words. "I will always have your back, that's why I'm saying this. I know it ain't easy for either of you, but it's gonna land you in prison."

"That's the only way I'll stop." I pat him on the back and head for the ring.

The fight lasts five minutes. I went in too full of rage at the thought of losing my ol' lady forever, and the next thing I know, my opponent's out cold on the ring floor. I grab my cash, knock back a whiskey that Cooper holds out to me, and we head back to the club.

Mila eyes my cut knuckles. "Let me clean those up," she mutters, pulling up a stool and placing a bowl of water by her feet. I don't bother to refuse because she wouldn't listen. She soaks some gauze in the bowl and then gently takes my hand, dabbing lightly at the fresh cuts.

"I miss her too," she finally says with a sad smile.

"I can't stop," I mumble, wincing with each swipe of the gauze. "When I'm not around her, I can't see straight. Without her, there's no point."

Her head shoots up, her eyes meeting mine. "What are you talking about, Tanner?"

"Nothing, forget it." If she tells Cooper what I've said, he'll have me sectioned for sure, but it's how I feel. I don't want to be here without her.

The main door opens and Lacey, one of the club girls, saunters in. On seeing me, she freezes. "Oh, you aren't usually here," she mutters.

Melissa almost runs into her back. "Lace, what the hell?" She laughs, and then she also spots me. "Stranger," she greets me with a smile.

"What is she doing here, Lacey?" snaps Mila.

"She had nowhere to go. I ran it past the Pres," explains Lacey with a shrug.

"Oh really," mutters Mila angrily. "We'll see about that." I watch as she stomps towards Cooper's office.

Melissa sits on the stool that Mila's vacated. She takes my swollen hand in hers and exams it. "Ouch, looks painful," she says, pressing a finger over one of my knuckles. I pull my hand free, scowling at her.

"What happened to wherever you were living?" I ask, realising I have no clue where or who she lives with.

"Well, thanks to you, I had to go back to my parents and now they've had enough of me. Lacey said she could help me out for a few days."

"You have parents?" I ask in surprise. Most of the club girls are estranged from their families. It's how they end up here looking for a replacement family.

She grins. "Of course, I do. Everyone has parents somewhere."

"What do they think of . . ." I trail off, pointing a finger at her rounded stomach.

"They were pissed. I'm their only daughter. I've just turned twenty and I'm pregnant by a biker who's probably old enough to be my dad."

"I'm not that old. Twenty-nine."

"Jeez," she says, shaking her head, "that's pretty old to me." When I don't reply, she picks up the gauze and begins to wipe my hand just like Mila did. "I'm sorry about everything. I know you're missing Brook." My shoulders tense. "I wish I could take back that night. We were both pretty wasted."

We haven't really discussed that night, and quite honestly, I've tried to forget the very few vague memories I have of it. "Did I come on to you?" One minute, I was drinking with the guys, and the next, I woke next to Melissa with no memory of the bits in between.

"I think we were both a little flirty. I probably took the lead, though. I usually do." I frown at her words, It doesn't sound like me. I'm the kind of guy to take the lead, especially in the bedroom, so hearing that she probably took over and I let her surprises me. Not only that, but I never flirt. It's just not me.

"Did I call you Brook?" I ask, slightly embarrassed. I refuse to believe I knowingly cheated—I must have thought it was Brook.

Mel shrugs again. "Maybe. I don't remember." She places her hand on my knee and gives it a gentle squeeze. "We need to talk about what's going to happen next, Tanner."

My eyes fall to her stomach. She sits up straighter and carefully places my hand over it. I close my eyes, wanting to snatch it back, because whatever's in there scares the shit out of me. It moves, and my eyes widen in surprise. "He's a real mover," she says with a smile. I feel another kick, and instead of feeling repulsed, I find myself willing it to move again. "Three months and he'll be here."

"He?" I repeat, and she nods, smiling.

"I have scan pictures when you're ready to see them. Yah know, I have no clue how to look after a kid. I've never even held a baby." She smiles nervously, and I feel bad for her. I got her in this state, and she's just as worried about it as me.

"I've been ignoring you, hoping it'll all go away," I admit. "I haven't thought about what comes next. Have you got all the baby stuff you need?" She's been taking money and always tells me it's for baby things.

Melissa shifted uneasily. "Not exactly. The money you gave me went to food and places to stay."

I feel more guilty. She's young and pregnant, and the last thing she should be thinking about is where she's gonna lay her head for the night. "I'll speak to Pres. We have loads of rooms here."

"Really?" she asks brightly. I nod, and she flings her arms around my neck, pressing herself against me. The baby kicks, and we both gasp, then smile. There's no reason why we shouldn't get along for his sake and I can't keep ignoring this mess I've made.

Brook

I've been on my feet eight hours straight so far. The weekend flew past, bringing Monday around far quicker than I'd wanted.

The salon's been busy all day, and I can't wait to get home and sink into a hot both. I sweep the last of the hair into a neat pile. "Are you coming for a drink, Brook?" asks James, and I shake my head. The after-work drinks are getting a bit too regular and my liver needs a break.

"Did you hear anything else from your ex after he turned up at the bar on Friday night?" asks Blake.

"He was at my apartment when I got home," I say. "We talked, and he left. He's just having trouble accepting it, but he'll move on eventually."

"You're crazy. I wouldn't let him move on. Seeing that hunk of a man with another woman would kill me," says Blake.

Just knowing Tanner touched another woman kills me—I didn't need to see it. I start tidying my workstation to distract myself. I can feel their eyes on me, but I don't explain because I can't stand to see their pity. My new friends don't know much about my past relationship, and I want to keep it that way. When I'm with Mila or Harper, it's all we talk about, and I don't want the same to happen here. Tanner consumes enough of my thoughts already.

"Are you okay to lock up?" Blake asks, and I give a nod. The others left early today, so it's only me, her, and James left.

"Of course. You guys get off, the bar is calling." I don't have to ask them twice—they have their jackets on before I can change my mind.

As I lock up, I realise that I haven't felt Tanner all day. I glance around and nothing seems out of place, but he's definitely not around. It's the first time since I left the club I've felt alone, and there's something sad about that. Maybe Cooper finally got through to him.

When I get back to my apartment, I'm surprised to find Mila sitting in the lobby, clutching a bottle of wine. She looks up at me and smiles, wiggling the wine. "Sorry to just turn up. I had to get away from my crazy life for a few hours."

I smile, pushing the button for the elevator. "You'd better come up then."

I shower quickly and change into my pyjamas. Mila is already curled up on my comfy couch with a glass of wine in her hand. "So, spill," I say, flopping down beside her and taking my glass from the coffee table. "What's happening in your life?"

She sighs. "I love my kids, I really do, but I don't like them very much today." She winces. "Does that make me a bad person?"

I laugh. "It makes you human."

"Noah just doesn't want to sleep lately. I'm sure it's just his teeth coming, but still, an hour would be nice. Of course, Cooper never seems to hear him wake up. Asher is being a pain at school. Every time I go to collect him, I'm hauled in to see his teacher. Again, Cooper is always too busy to do the pick-up. I swear, if I hear the excuse 'club business' again, I might kill him."

I squeeze her hand sympathetically. "Oh Mila, it sounds full-on. What's wrong with Asher?"

Mila shrugs. "I'm not sure. Since the adoption became official, I feel like he's testing the water a little. Maybe it's just his age. I'm sure he'll settle down."

"He will. He has great parents."

"Listen to me moaning on. How are you?" Without realising it, she gives me the pitying look, and so I plaster on a smile.

"I'm good. Work is amazing, and I met a guy on Friday. He's a banker." I fail to mention that I haven't called him to arrange that date.

"Wow, that's great news, Brook. You're really getting your life together." Her smile fades. "We all miss you so much at the club. Even Sam is sad."

"I know. I miss you guys too, but it is what it is."

"Tanner should have to leave, not you. I hate that he's there when you aren't. I had a huge fight with Cooper last night because of him."

"Mila, please don't argue with Cooper over me and Tanner."

"He's letting Melissa stay at the club . . ." She trails off and waits for my reaction.

I can't deny it hurts. My chest feels tight and I want to cry, but I force it back. Melissa is taking my place, and soon, the guys won't even think about me because she'll be Tanner's ol' lady and I'll be no one. I shrug. "Well, I guess it makes sense. She is having his baby, and that means it's a club baby." It hits me that it's also the reason he isn't watching me anymore.

"You sound like Cooper. You were seventeen when you came to the club, and you've been there ever since. That's a huge chunk of your life, and I don't see why you should be pushed out because he fucked it all up." Mila begins to cry, and I take her hands in mine.

"Please don't get upset. I chose to leave. Cooper told me I didn't have to go, but I wanted to. I needed to see what was beyond the club. It's all I've ever really known for my whole adult life, and it was time for me to fly the nest."

"Well, now you've seen what's beyond the walls, you need to come home. We're your family, and I know it hurts that you can't have kids, but being a part of the club means you get to be a mum to everyone's kids, husbands, whoever you want." She throws her arms up in the air. "Our kids love you. You're like their second mum. Harper agrees, all the ol' ladies do, and we want you home. If you were there, you'd help me with Asher's school and Noah's sleeping issues."

I smile. She's right, I would. "You're doing amazing. You don't need me."

"Are you okay with Melissa moving in?" she wails, crying harder.

"I don't know how I feel, to be honest. It hurts. Today was the first day I didn't feel him around. He's moving on, but I guess that's what I wanted, right?"

"Is it?" she queries. "What did he say to you on Friday?"

I give a small, unhappy laugh. "He offered to give me a baby." I shake my head. "Donor or part-time daddy, the choice is mine."

Mila gasps, her eyes wide. "Wow, what a turn-around. What happened to him not wanting kids?"

"Guilt speaks volumes. He can stick his baby. I waited long enough, and he gave it to someone else just like that. I wonder if Melissa knows he's offering out his sperm?" I laugh, and Mila makes a puking sound.

"I still can't believe he did this to you, Brook. It just doesn't seem real."

"Life is full of surprises."

CHAPTER THREE

Tanner

"No, not like that. You have to rub it hard," groans Melissa, wiggling her arse. I sigh, placing more pressure on her back. She's on all fours on her bed, her backside in the air and her face buried in a pillow. "Oh yeah, that's good, right there," she moans. I adjust my pants. It's so inappropriate to get hard while massaging the woman I got into this state, but it's been months since I've had sex and seeing her round, perky arse in the air like this is causing involuntary reactions. She rolls onto her side and lifts her top. "I think he enjoyed it." She points to a movement under her skin, and I peer closer. "Feel," she adds, making a grab for my hand.

"I shouldn't. I . . ." I trail off, but it's pointless trying to hide the erection that's clearly creating a tent in my joggers.

"Oh," she says, her eyes falling to it. "Wow."

"Yeah, I'm sorry about that. I should go," I stammer, heading for the door.

"We could sort it if you like." She smirks, and I freeze with my hand on the doorknob. I glance back, and she winks seductively.

"It's not a good idea," I mutter, pulling the door open and rushing out.

I jump on my motorbike and somehow end up here. It proves my head is all kinds of messed up lately. Lighting a cigarette, I inhale deeply and cast my eyes over the run-down building. I once called it home, and it's exactly how I remember it. The walls inside hold fucked-up memories for me, ones that I've pushed deep down for years.

A car drives past slowly with the windows down and music blaring out. I'm in dangerous territory—these streets are owned by gangs, and being an unknown face in this area is asking for trouble. I flick my cigarette onto the ground and crush it under my heavy boot, and then I move towards the house.

The garden is overgrown, but it's always been that way. Most of the houses on this row are the same, so it doesn't stand out. I climb the steps, taking in the broken terracotta plant pots on the porch. As I raise my fist to knock, the door swings open. Looking down into the eyes of my mother brings all kinds of emotions to the surface and I swallow hard. I didn't expect to feel much, maybe not anything, but here I am getting all choked and shit.

"Carl," she breathes, her voice unsure.

"Ma," I mumble.

"Oh my god, I can't believe you're here." She brushes her small hands down the front of her apron. "Well, come on inside." She steps back, letting me pass. "How have you been? It's, what, three years since I saw you last?"

Inside hasn't changed much either. The walls and furniture are dated back to the seventies, and the couch is worn and almost threadbare. "I've been okay. You? Where's Dad?"

Her expression changes at the mention of him. My mum has always been tired-looking. She's never worn makeup or had nice clothes. Everything was second-hand from charity shops. It was my dad's fault—he's a drunk and has been for many years. "Oh, you know your father, he comes and goes. I haven't seen him for around a week or so. Last I heard, he was seeing some young girl. Pathetic, really . . ." She trails off, dusting some imaginary fluff from her shirt. His other flaw—he likes younger women. It doesn't matter, though. My mum will still take him back when he decides to come home again. The cycle has been the same for my entire life. It's one of the reasons I joined the Forces at seventeen, so I could escape their toxic relationship. "How's Brooky?" I hate the nickname my mum uses, but Brook always thought it was cute.

"We aren't together. We split up about three months ago."

She gasps and clutches her hands over her heart. "But you two were inseparable. What happened?"

"It just didn't work out. Are you okay for money now Dad's gone?" A change of subject is needed. I don't want to explain the whole thing to her, to have her looking at me with disappointment, thinking I've become just like my dad.

"I'm fine. I clean a few of the house on this street for extra money. Miss Hadley was asking me about you just the other day, in fact." She smiles. "Tea?" I nod. It's no good asking for a whiskey in this house, since she refuses to bring alcohol here because of Dad.

"I can give you some if you need extra," I offer.

She shakes her head. "No need, you keep it. Maybe send Brooky some flowers. Girls like a grand gesture." I laugh to myself. Only my mum would see a bunch of flowers as a grand gesture. "What did you do, Carl?" Her tone has switched to serious as she hands me my tea.

"It's not important," I mutter.

"You cheated?" And when I don't respond, she groans. "Carl, you of all people! I knew Brooky wouldn't have left without good reason."

"Her name is Brook, Ma, stop calling her Brooky. I know I fucked up. I don't need you to tell me that, okay."

"I'm just disappointed. I know how much she meant to you, and I can't get my head around you doing something like that. Is she okay?"

"What do you think? She hates me. She's moved out from the club and got herself an apartment, a new job. She's got this whole other life that doesn't involve me."

"Are you giving her space?" she asks, raising her eyebrow.

"What's that supposed to mean?" I snap.

"I know how you can be, and I know how obsessed you were with her. Are you leaving her alone? Maybe she just needs time away to miss you?"

"No, Ma, it's past that. The other girl is pregnant. There's no way Brook can forgive me for that."

"Oh son, poor Brook." She places her tea on the table. "Is this other girl in your life now?"

I shake my head. "Not like that. She's around the club because she doesn't have a place just yet, but we aren't together. I don't want the kid, and she knows that, but I guess my feelings don't matter."

She scoffs. "Carl Tanner, you need to step up. This is your chance to be a good father. I know you can do better than the one I lumbered us both with."

"I doubt that." I drink the rest of my tea and place the cup down. "I should go."

"Will you come back soon? I've missed seeing you." A bang on the front door interrupts us, and my mum looks panic-stricken. "That might be your father. Go out the back."

She tries to bustle me to the kitchen door, but I stand firm. "No, he'll have seen my motorbike anyway. That's probably why he's here." I pull open the front door and a man I recognise as my father is slumped against the porch. He looks older, but he's still a big motherfucker, which is surprising given the amount he drinks. I can't imagine he sees the gym much. He looks up as I step out and then laughs to himself.

"Thought that was your bike out there. What the fuck are you doing back?"

"I came to see Ma."

"After years of staying away. Bernice, hasn't it been three years?" he yells to my mum.

She stands behind me and gives my arm a gentle squeeze. "What's it matter? He's here now."

"What's he after?"

"What could I get from you?" I ask, laughing coldly. "Where have you been anyway? Ma said you haven't been around, but I'm guessing you weren't far if you saw my motorbike. Are you fucking on your own doorstep these days?"

"Fuck you," he slurs, trying to stand but failing.

My mum sighs. "That's enough. You go, Carl, and don't leave it so long next time."

I nod. "You know you can come to me anytime, Ma. You're always welcome at the club."

"She wouldn't step foot in there with you criminals," Dad spits. I roll my eyes, knowing he's just bitter because he wasn't accepted into the Hammers when Cooper and Kain's dad's set it up.

I head for my bike, ignoring the drunken prick, and wonder for the millionth time why my mum doesn't leave him.

Brook

It was nice catching up with Mila. It's times like this that leave me missing the club and everyone there. They were my family. She also invited me to a barbecue at the club. They often have huge parties and open up to the local community, but I knew when I told her I'd think it over that I wouldn't be going. Not now I know Melissa is living there.

I slip down deeper into the bathtub, letting the water soak my hair and groaning as the heat eases my aching muscles. It's hard work at the salon, and I still have so much to learn. I hadn't prepared myself for the long hours being on my feet. I've been toying with the idea of going to college, thinking maybe I need a new career.

Eventually, I pull myself out of the tub and wrap a towel around my hair. I catch a glimpse of my naked self in the bathroom mirror and gasp. I look too thin, and my ribs are visible. There are dark circles under my eyes, and my face appears older than it should. "Girl, you have got to start eating," I mumble out loud as I go into my bedroom.

"I agree," the low tone of Tanner's voice catches me off guard and I scream, making him wince.

"How the hell did you get in here?" I yell, turning on the light. I inhale sharply. Tanner's face is beaten and bloody, as are his hands.

"Cover up or I won't be able to stop myself," he mumbles. He's kicked off his boots and is laying back against the headboard of my bed. "In fact, don't. I should have to stare at you, to see what the hell I lost."

I grab for a shirt and pull it on. "What happened?"

"Fight," he shrugs. "I finally lost."

"A fight where, at the club?" He shakes his head, his eyes drifting closed.

"Oh lord," I mumble. "Carl Tanner, don't you dare go to sleep on my bed." I sit beside him, gently tapping his cheek to wake him. He opens one eye and smiles, showing his teeth are bloody. "I'll call Cooper to come get you."

Tanner's hand snatches my wrist, and he holds it firm. "No. Give me five minutes and I'll be on my way. I just needed the noise to stop for a while." His eyes close again, and I groan. I'm not strong enough to have him so near. If he touches me, I'm too weak to say no. And besides, I don't want him bleeding all over my fresh, clean bedding.

I gather some medical supplies from the bathroom and then perch next to him on my bed. He's asleep, or concussed, I'm unsure which. It's not the first time I've cleaned him up after a fight, but these times were less as we got older. In the early days, when he was trying to prove himself to the club and make us some money, he'd do cage fighting night after night, and I'd cry every time he came home hurt. I hated those days.

I drop some gauze into the mix of water and antiseptic and then gently press it to his busted lip. His eyes shoot open as he hisses. "Don't be a baby," I whisper with a smile.

"Brook?" He looks confused. "What are you doing here?"

"You came to my place, although I don't know how the hell you got in here." I huff. "I chose this apartment because of the security, and here you are, sitting on my bed like you damn well belong," I mutter as I wipe at his cuts.

"Baby, I miss you." He sighs, keeping his eyes closed. "So fucking much, it hurts."

"Tanner, don't. I'm cleaning you up, and then you have to go." He nods, but I'm not stupid enough to think he'll just leave when the five minutes are up.

I finish cleaning him up and then rub some healing balm into his knuckles. He's asleep again, his light snores tugging at my heart strings. He used to say he could only sleep when we were together, and I wonder how much he's slept since I left. I sigh, pulling a blanket over him. Maybe sleep is what he needs to gain a new focus and clear his head. I'm disappointed in myself for looking after him when he doesn't deserve it, but at least he's too injured to try his luck, cos Lord knows I might cave, and then I would be pissed at myself.

I look one last time at his peaceful but bruised face and turn out the light. A few hours won't hurt. I settle down on the couch and drift to sleep thinking of Tanner and how sad and alone he looks.

I inhale sharply and my eyes spring open. It takes me a second to realise I'm on the couch and a further minute to realise the dream I'd been having of Tanner working his hands over my body is in fact real and not a dream at all. "Don't say it. Don't say anything," he whispers, resting his forehead against my own.

"Tanner, please," I whisper back. I'm not sure if I'm begging him to stop or to carry on. He presses his lips cautiously against mine. Something inside me clicks, and I grip his face in my hands and kiss him back with so much ferocity, it surprises us both. He eventually breaks the kiss, breathing heavily as he nuzzles into my neck, nipping the delicate skin the way I've always loved. His kisses begin to descend down my body, past my navel and across my hip. As he tugs down my pink lace underwear, all sane thoughts have left my head and I lift my hips, giving him a silent go-ahead.

Tanner's movements are hurried and jerky. He runs his tongue along the inside of my thigh and then very lightly brushes it over my opening. I freeze, my mind racing with reasons not to go ahead with this, but before I can voice any one of them, Tanner buries his face between my legs. He sucks and licks every inch of my pussy until I cry out, gripping his hair in my hands to pull him closer.

"Oh shit, Tanner," I pant. I can feel the waves crashing over me, consuming me. It's been too long since I've had an orgasm from anything other than my battery-operated friend, and my reaction is loud and so very unlike me. As I flop back onto the couch, my breathing rapid, my only thought is to have Tanner inside me. I need to feel him in me, on me.

He moves up my body and rests himself between my open legs, keeping his weight on his elbows. "Remember when I did that outside the clubhouse? You were laid on my motorbike dressed in black lace and heels. I didn't care that we might get caught, I had to taste you," he whispers, kissing me gently. I wriggle beneath him impatiently. I don't want to take a trip down memory lane—I need something else from him.

He smirks, his cut lip lopsided from swelling. "I'm sorry I turned up like this. Here . . ." He dangles a key in front of me. "I waited for another resident to come in, that's how I got in the main door downstairs. I also stole your spare key last time I came here." He presses it into my hand and then kisses me on the forehead and rises to his feet. "Goodnight, baby."

"What?" I gasp, pulling myself to sit up. "You're leaving?"

"You've been more than generous letting me sleep for a few hours, and I appreciate that. You have no idea how much I needed it."

I watch him walk towards the door and then scramble to my feet, rushing after him, "But I . . ."

He stops and turns to me. "What?"

I feel silly telling him I want him to carry on. I've left him, he cheated, and now, I'm practically begging him to fuck me. I shake my head. "Never mind. Keep those wounds clean and stay out of fights."

Tanner smiles, nodding. "See yah, Brook." Then, he's gone, and I'm left feeling sad and alone . . . again.

CHAPTER FOUR

Tanner

I feel lighter than I have in months. It was hard leaving Brook like that last night, but I knew she'd regret it when she's thinking clearly again, and I don't want her to hate me any more than she already does. I shovel more scrambled eggs into my mouth, looking up as Melissa comes into the kitchen carrying Willow in her arms. I pause mid-chew. "Does Harper know you have her kid?" The ol' ladies are far from wanting to forgive me or Mel for what we've done to Brook.

"Relax, big guy. Kain just shoved her in my arms and said he'd be a minute. He looked like he was in a rush."

"That means she doesn't know. Give her here," I huff, and Mel passes the six-month-old to me. Willow grips my beard, giving me a gummy grin. It isn't often that kids like me, especially this young, but Willow always smiles for me.

"They're gonna have to get used to me being around. I'm practically one of them now," sighs Mel, taking my fork and stealing some of my eggs.

"No, you ain't, and trust me, those ol' ladies can hold a grudge," I say, frowning at her as she slides my plate closer and takes a seat beside me.

"Who made these eggs?" She moans, closing her eyes with pleasure.

"Lacey. She'll make a great ol' lady. Us bikers like a woman who can cook," I hint. Melissa hasn't lifted a finger in the kitchen, or anywhere else for that matter, and the other women are getting pissed. Everyone has to pull their weight around here.

"Hell will freeze over before you catch me in a kitchen cooking for any man," she quips.

"Cooper won't let you stay for long if you don't pull your weight around the club, Mel. The point of a club girl is that you do shit like cook and clean. Sex with the guys is a bonus," I say. Melissa prefers to sit around the place gossiping with Lacey.

"I'm having your baby, so that makes me a step up from a club girl," she snaps.

"You came here months ago knowing the deal, and looking back, I don't remember you doing much then either. Everyone who stays here, pays their way. If that's by cooking, cleaning, or fucking, then that's what you do, so pick one and get on with it," I say, shaking my head. I don't know who the hell she thinks she is, trying to get a free ride. Even the ol' ladies help out.

"I choose fucking," she smirks, "so anytime you need me, just let me know."

"Me and you," I snap, pointing back and forth between us, "ain't ever gonna happen again."

I think back to the last time I said those exact words to her. I'd been balls deep inside Brook, my favourite place to be, and my phone had beeped over and over with text messages. Eventually, Brook had sighed and pushed me from her, saying, "Answer the damn messages. It's clearly important." I'd spent so much time since then wishing she hadn't made me look at those messages. It wouldn't have changed the outcome, but if I'd known what was about to unravel, I'd have spent longer buried inside her, taking my time to enjoy every second we had left.

The messages had been from Melissa. I'd even saved her damn name under 'Mistake' because it's what she was. But her messages sounded urgent, demanding I meet her, otherwise she'd come and find me and tell Brook what had happened between us. I was frustrated with the whole situation because Melissa hadn't taken the hints. Instead, she'd flirted continuously with me, even when Brook was in the same room, which was most of the time. At one point, she'd sat on my lap and rubbed her ass against me like a damn stripper. Luckily, Brook at been at the bar with her back to us.

Anyway, I went to the meeting point, some woods nearby the club. Melissa was sat on a tree stump, her hood pulled over her head, and I remember thinking that she looked like a sulky teenager, the reality being that's exactly what she was. When I demanded to know what the fuck she wanted so urgently, she'd looked at me with red, swollen eyes and tears running down her pale face, and she'd said, "I don't know what to do, Tanner. We've fucked up."

I was so pissed I'd left my ol' lady's bed for that bullshit and told her as much, and that's when her devastating words came tumbling out. The words that turned my whole world upside down. *I'm pregnant*. It'd taken me a few minutes to process it, and once I'd come to my senses, I tried to deny the kid was even mine. It got ugly and we argued until eventually she threatened me. She told me in no uncertain terms that I wasn't making any decisions about the kid. It was her body, her choice. She also made it clear that unless I kept her happy, she'd be going right to Brook with the whole sordid tale. And then I did something I'd never done before—I grabbed her by the throat, pushed her up against a tree, and got in her face. When I think about that now, I shudder in disgust, but the threat of losing Brook was all too real, and I was terrified, desperate even. I'd spat the words, "You're making a mistake, little girl. Do you know who the fuck I am and what these hands are capable of? I could snap your neck now and no fucker would know."

But Melissa wasn't fazed, she stared me right in the eye and smirked. "You think I've kept this secret to myself? If I'm not in contact with my friend soon, she'll call the Police and send them here, and then she'll put a call into that innocent little fairy you call your wife. Now, get your fucking hands off me." Then, she'd lightly traced her finger over my chest with heat in her eyes and a grin wider than the Channel Tunnel. She had the upper hand, and we both fucking knew it.

I'd gripped her tiny wrist, halting her hand from wandering any farther. "Let's get one thing straight, me and you, we ain't gonna happen again."

I must have sat in those woods for hours thinking of ways to break the news to Brook, but I couldn't come up with one where she didn't kick my arse to the kerb. Looking back, it would have been better coming from me. Instead, I was a coward, and Melissa eventually did the deed. I don't think I've ever seen pain in someone's eyes like that, and Brook ain't ever looked at me properly since.

Melissa laughs, bringing me back into the room. It's not a humorous laugh but one full of resentment. "You landed me in this mess. Do I have to fuck your brothers with your baby in my belly?"

"Jesus, Mel, just wash a pot now and again, that's all I'm saying. Once the kid is here, you'll have to do a lot more around here. If you can't cook, how the hell are you gonna take care of a kid?"

"Can you cook?" she snaps back. "Why do women have to do all the shit jobs around here? I bet a man made up that rule. And I'll feed the kid take-out."

I inwardly groan. Brook was right—Mel is gonna make a terrible mum. "I do shit, I pull in money for the club, I work at the garage when I'm needed, and I even work the bar if shit needs doing."

"So, the men go and do man jobs and us women have to stay back here chained to the kitchen sink? I don't think so. Times have changed, and while I have your kid, you'll need to cough up the cash."

"And what exactly are you gonna do to provide for this kid?" I snap.

She stands, a grin pulling at her lips. "I'll be raising it."

"Yeah, you're happy to play a woman's role when it comes to that part," I mutter, rolling my eyes. I watch her as she waddles from the room. Willow smiles at me again, and I place a gentle kiss on her head, then she giggles at my beard tickling her. Maybe I won't be such a bad dad, especially if my kid is anything like Willow. And Lord knows, that kid's gonna need all the help it can get with Mel as its mother.

Kain saunters into the room, taking Willow from me. He sighs before muttering, "Harper has gone to the salon to have her hair done, and get this, she reckons she'll be gone for hours. I blame you!"

"Me?" I ask, confused.

"Yes. Brook always did that shit for the ol' ladies. Now, they need to go to the salon, which not only costs stupid money but we get left with the kids. Remember back when all this shit hit the fan, I told you to keep quiet, not to tell Brook what a dick you'd been, and what did you do?"

"You did what?" Harper's voice rings out around the kitchen. Kain keeps his back to her, his expression frozen in fear. "I asked you a question."

"Babe, I thought you'd left," he replies, pasting on a bright smile and turning slowly to face her.

"You told him not to tell Brook? You knew about it, and you told him to keep it a secret?" Harper looks shocked and then her expression changes to sadness. "And you lied to me too."

"I didn't lie to you, baby," says Kain calmly.

"But you didn't tell me about it," she points out, "so technically, you lied. You kept secrets."

"But we weren't together then, not properly," he explains, sounding desperate. "And when we woke up and saw Tanner and Mel, we were all shocked, even Tanner."

Harper's expression changes again, this time to rage. "You were with him when it happened?" I wince at Kain's runaway mouth and its ability to cause more shit with each word. "You and who? What did you mean by we?"

"Harper, you're blowing this out of proportion," he tries, glancing back at me for support. I shrug. It's gone too far to salvage.

"Cooper. Of course, it was Cooper. Explain, because I'm lost, did you have an orgy?" she hisses.

"Christ, no, I slept on the floor. I didn't even know he'd done anything. We were passed out drunk."

"You wait until I tell Mila about this," she growls.

"Baby, you can't tell Mila. Cooper will have my balls. Why are you acting all crazy and shit? Did you get your period early?"

My eyes widen around the same time that Harper's mouth falls open. "You stupid idiot," I mumble from behind him. How can anyone fuck up so badly with words?

"I'm going to get my hair done, then I'll come back for the kids. We'll be sleeping at home tonight. You can stay here and sleep on the damn floor with your lying, cheating friends." She stomps from the room. Willow begins to cry, and Kain holds her closer, rocking her and placing kisses on her head.

"What the hell just happened?" he asks, sounding confused.

I glare at him in exasperation. "You opened that stupid mouth of yours and out came shit that should have stayed buried. Do you see why lying never works, Kain? Your mouth is a liability. It was always gonna come back to bite us."

Harper's true to her word. She called Mila and told her everything, which resulted in Mila screaming at Cooper before storming out.

I glance beside me at Kain and then Cooper, each of us nursing a whiskey and staring blankly into our glasses. "I don't understand how you got to fuck up with a pretty, nineteen-year-old pussy, yet we're all being punished." Kain sighs.

"It's your fault, yah clown." I laugh, swirling the ice in my drink. "Speaking of pussy, the guys are bored of Lacey, and Melissa is out of action for a few months. We need to find some new women. You guys forget about us single brothers just because you're married."

"Haven't you learnt from Melissa, brother? These women are dangerous. I don't want shit like that happening again, not in my club. And these days, it's hard to find a woman who wants to come in and look after a bunch of bikers. There're no old-fashioned women out there anymore. They all want to work and earn their own money. It's all about independence," says Cooper.

"Tell me about it. Melissa had a shit fit today when I talked about her doing more around here to earn her keep. Apparently, that's what I'm here for."

"Gold diggers," Kain sighs again, "the struggle is real."

"Did we even run checks on Melissa when she first came? Who vouched for her?" I ask.

"She knew Ginger," mutters Kain. Ginger was his ex who died after giving birth to his son, Kian.

"So, you vouched for her?" I ask.

"No, not really. She just started hanging around the bar, and I think one of the guys got her back here one night. Rumours about her fucking on the pool table spring to mind, but I don't remember who she fucked. Maybe Woody and Marshall?" he replies vaguely. "Anyhow, it's a little late for you to question her intentions now she's pregnant with your kid. Gold digger or not, you're stuck with her."

"Do I need to make her my ol' lady?" I ask, hating each word as it spills from my mouth.

Cooper shrugs. "Without the title, she ain't shit around here, man. You know that. She's fair game and unprotected if she fucks up. If she doesn't pull her weight once the kid is here, I'll have to question if she can stay. The club can't afford to take in strays, brother." I nod, already knowing the rules.

"You could always buy a house. Keep her separate from club business," suggests Kain. The idea had crossed my mind. Both Cooper and Kain have houses off-site, which means their ol' ladies and kids can catch a break from the club life. I'd never bothered to do that with Brook because she loved being here at the club. She loved the guys like brothers, and they loved her equally as much.

Brook

It was a surprise to get home and find Mila in the lobby again, but this time, she has Harper with her too. "Two nights running. Do your husbands know where you're at?" I smile.

"Oh honey, they're too scared to even question us right now. We need wine and food, so get changed cos we're taking you out," says Mila, her tone no-nonsense, which means I won't get out of this, not even with the excuse that I'm shattered from another long day at the salon.

"You'd better come up while I get changed," I suggest, pressing the call button for the elevator.

TANNER

Mila booked us a table at a small Italian place a few streets from my apartment. It's authentic, with the small tables, white and red checked cloths, and low lights hanging, giving the place a warm glow.

The girls take turns filling me in on what Harper overheard earlier today. I can't deny that it hurts, as it's betrayal from the men I considered my brothers. I take a deep breath and smile. "I'm sure they just wanted to prevent all the drama, and Tanner is their brother, so they'd always have his back over anyone's. I get it."

"No, don't do that. Don't excuse what they did. They were out of order," snaps Mila.

"Like we wouldn't have done the same? In fact, we have done that. When you spotted Jase with another woman, I told you not to tell Kayla. Sometimes, nothing good comes from it. I'm glad I found out, and I wish it had of come from Tanner himself rather than her, but we can't change the past. We have to move on."

Mila sighs heavily. "Doesn't make it right, though."

"In other news, Tanner turned up in my apartment last night," I announce. Both girls turn to me wide-eyed.

"Again?" asks Harper, and I nod.

"He stole my spare key the first time and used it last night to let himself in. He was beat up pretty bad. Any idea what happened?"

Mila shakes her head and shrugs. "Sometimes the guys get into fights, but I was at the club last night and nothing happened. In fact, it was pretty quiet. Didn't he say what happened?"

"Nope, just that it was a fight."

"Why are you looking concerned? Don't you go worrying about him. He's his own worst enemy," snaps Harper. "I hope you kicked him out."

"Not exactly," I say with a guilty expression. "He went to sleep in my bed, and so I left him there. I thought that rest might do him good."

Mila eyes me suspiciously. "And?"

"And I slept on the couch," I reply then take a few big gulps of wine.

"And?" pushes Harper, not falling for my innocent act.

"And he went down on me." I rush the words out, regretting it instantly when both women stare at me with horrified expressions.

"No!" screeches Harper, and I wince, nodding.

"You gave in and let him worm his way back into your knickers!" hisses Mila.

"I was weak." I groan, placing my head in my hands. "The worst thing was, I almost begged him to carry on," I confess.

"Wait a minute, so he went down on you and then just left?" asked Mila.

"Yeah, weird, right? But at least he had more self-control than me." From the second he left, I was ashamed. I'd been so easy to let him touch me after everything he's done, and then I laid awake for hours wondering if he left me to fuck her. Was he feeling guilty about cheating on her? "Anyway, it got me thinking. I need to make everything more final between us." I pause, going over the words to make sure I'm one hundred percent sure before I say them aloud. "I saw my solicitor at lunch today, and he drew up my divorce papers."

Harper whistles. "That is pretty final."

"Are you sure?" asks Mila, looking concerned.

"Yeah, I guess it's the next step. After you told me about Melissa moving into the clubhouse, I felt he'd made his choice, and I know that contradicts what happened last night, but maybe that was my way of letting go. Or maybe I just felt a sick satisfaction that he came to me when he was hurt and not her." I shrug. "Either way, I've made my choice. I want to give them to Tanner myself, to soften the blow."

"I'll pre-warn Cooper. You might need the guys around just in case he explodes," suggests Mila.

CHAPTER FIVE

Tanner

The week flies by, and I've been avoiding the clubhouse as much as possible. It's no fun when Mila and Harper are still upset with the guys—the atmosphere is too cold. So, here I am, spending my Friday night enjoying my favourite pastime, watching Brook. I check my watch. It's almost ten in the evening, and she's in a bar I know well, chatting with some jumped-up guy in a suit. He doesn't look like her type. He's tall and willowy with beady eyes, but who knows what her type is these days. Every time I see her, I notice slight changes, like how she wears heels over flats, even during the daytime, and she favours wool sweaters rather than her usual hooded ones. There're no more cute cotton dresses, as they've been replaced with jeans, and she's even taken to tying her hair back. I always liked her to wear it loose.

I drink the last drop of coffee from my Styrofoam cup and head over to the well-lit bar, dropping the cup in the rubbish bin as I pass. Once inside, instead of storming over to Brook, like every fibre of my being wants me to, I head for the bar. I know the owner here, so I can pretend this is purely coincidence.

There're hardly any customers, and I wonder how Tom keeps this place running if this is his usual Friday night. I watch as he throws a cocktail shaker in the air, his customer watching in awe. He pours the contents into a large glass and slides it to her in some kind of Tom Cruise move, and then he makes his way over to me. "Tanner, man, long time no see," he says loudly, slapping my hand in greeting.

I feel Brook's eyes reach me, but I pay no attention, pretending I haven't noticed her.

"Tom, still pulling out your best moves, I see. Pretty smooth." I laugh, taking a seat on a barstool. Tom served in the Armed Forces around the same time as me. He was injured in a blast near Kabul, and the payout he received for that paid for this bar.

"You know it, brother. You just can't hide it when you look this good." He grabs a bottle of Scotch and sets down two glasses in front of me. "What brings you to my bar?"

"I'm watching the female over there by the window. Don't give the game away, I'm pretending I haven't seen her," I say in a hushed voice.

"Pretty little thing. I noticed her as soon as she walked in. Why you watching her?"

"It's Brook," I say, swirling the Scotch around in my glass.

"Your Brook? Aren't you together no more?" I shake my head, taking a sip. "Wow, I can see why you claimed her, brother. She's better than you described."

"You know who she's with over there?"

"Yeah, he comes in here a lot. I think he goes to the University around here, he's often in here with the other students."

"Yeah, he looks like a geek," I observe. Tom tops up my glass and pats me on the shoulder before going back to serve the lone female farther along the bar.

"Is it a coincidence?" Brook's angry voice comes from behind me, and I smirk.

I glance back over my shoulder like I'm surprised. "Brook, hey," I say, keeping my voice neutral. "I'm just here to see an old friend."

"Really, cos you never saw friends when you were with me."

I turn back to my Scotch, putting my back to her. "I did. Not often, but I did."

"I guess there was a lot you did that I didn't know about," she mutters.

"Touché, Brook." I hear her huff. "Is it a date?" I ask, turning to look at her. She's already making her way back to the man.

"None of your business, Tanner," she says, halting halfway between us.

"It is when we're still married, baby. And when you still let me eat your pussy in the middle of the night," I point out, and she growls, marching back towards me again.

"Please don't do this to me. Harrison is helping me out with something, and I could do without you scaring him off."

"Desperate times, Brook," I quip, and she scowls. "Times must be hard if you have to choose someone like him. I can always help you out again," I add, winking.

"Seriously, Tanner, don't fuck this up for me."

"Tell me what he's helping you out with."

"Why do you want to know?" she demands, and I shrug. She groans. "Fine. I'm thinking of going back to university in the evenings."

It's not what I was expecting to hear. She'd never expressed any wishes to go out and get a career or go to uni. "That's great. To do what?"

"I haven't decided. I just know that hair isn't for me."

"But you always loved it."

"I used to, but it's not me anymore." I raise my eyebrows, and she scowls again, placing her hands on her hips. "What?"

"Nothing. I was just thinking how you've changed so much lately."

"It wasn't a choice. I had to." I watch her arse sway in her tight-fit jeans as she walks away. I should be pleased for her, but I feel left behind, like her life is suddenly taking off. Decisions like that were things she would have once spoken to me about, and now she's making all kinds of changes, it's hard to sit back and watch.

My mobile vibrates and Cooper's name flashes up. "What's up?" I answer, still watching Brook as she talks animatedly to the geek.

"Are you close by? Your mum's turned up at the club." I frown because my ma never comes to the club.

"On my way," I mutter, ending the call and chucking some screwed-up notes onto the bar. "Thanks, Tom. I have to split, something came up."

"No worries, man. Don't leave it so long next time."

I leave the bar without saying goodbye to Brook. It's petty, and I feel her eyes follow me from the bar, but I can't bring myself to be nice when I feel so distant from her. And as I make my way to my bike, I wonder if the pain in my chest is from the knowledge she's moved on with her life or because we're now acting like complete strangers.

"Ma," I greet her with a kiss to the cheek, my expression full of concern. She looks more tired and paler than usual.

"I'm so sorry to just turn up like this, Carl." She sighs, taking a cup of tea from Mila.

"That's okay. I told you that you were welcome here anytime."

"It's your father," she murmurs, lowering into a seat.

I take a seat opposite her, preparing myself in case she breaks the news he's dead. "Okay, what'd he do now?"

"He left me."

I let that sink in. I almost feel disappointed that the news hadn't been what I was expecting. "Right," I say, puzzled, because he's always leaving her, so it's nothing new or surprising.

"I mean for good. He took his stuff, and he's never done that before."

"Well, maybe he's just stepping up his game." I shrug, not feeling overly concerned.

She shakes her head. "No, this feels different. He's gone. That isn't why I came here, though. He was talking crazy, saying that everything was your fault."

"So, what's new, Ma," I say with a laugh. The drunken bastard blames everything on me, from his drinking problem to the fact that his friend abused me when I was a kid.

"He was talking about payback, Carl. You know how he gets, but this time, he said he was part of a plan to take you down and it was playing out right before our eyes. He seemed so focused, more than normal. I'm worried for you."

"Ma, honestly, take it as nothing. He's spent his life blaming me and telling me I'd pay, but yah know what, so far, he's done nothing. He's too lazy to get revenge. I'll make sure I'm on guard if it makes you feel better," I say with a smile. "Look, why don't you stay here tonight? We have loads of spare rooms."

She glances around the large living space. "Oh, I don't want to be a nuisance. There's a late bus."

"Ma, it's fine. Please stay, I'd like you to."

She smiles and gives a nod. "It is pretty lonely at home just lately."

Melissa makes her way over. "Shit, Tanner, I know you said we should get more ass in, but really?"

I roll my eyes. "Melissa, this is my mother," I mutter dryly, and her smile fades.

"Oh shit, sorry," she apologises. "I'm Mel."

"Ma, this is Melissa," I introduce her properly. "The woman I told you about."

"The mother of your unborn grandchild," adds Melissa, and I groan, glaring at her.

"Oh, you look nothing like Brook," my mum points out, almost sounding disappointed, and a laugh escapes me. My mum isn't stupid—she knows exactly what she's doing. She doesn't like Melissa, and this is her way of putting it out there. She favours Brook, just like everyone here does.

Mel runs her hand over her bump and shrugs. "No, but clearly I sucked his cock better," she says with a fake smile, before stomping away.

"Lovely girl," quips Mum, and I nod, grinning at her sarcasm.

"Sorry, I should have warned you about her. I think she's bi-polar or something. Crazy ass bitch runs her mouth off too much." I stare after Mel, thinking over her last comment.

Once Mum is settled, I march into Cooper's office without knocking. "I know you say you don't remember that night I fucked my life up, but Melissa just said something that threw me."

"I don't have time for your baby mama drama right now, Tanner, get the fuck out," Cooper growls.

"It's important, Pres. She said she sucked my cock," I blurt out.

"Fuck," Cooper growls, throwing his head back and gripping the arms on his chair. "Tanner, get out. I'm getting a little cock sucking myself, and you're ruining my moment." Mila's laughter rings out from under the desk.

I screw my face up in disgust. "You guys shouldn't be doing that shit when you have kids. Grow the fuck up," I snap, marching from the office and slamming the door for good measure.

Cooper's laughter follows me. "Don't be hating just cos you ain't got a good woman anymore," he yells after me.

Brook

It felt good to meet with Harrison. William had pointed me in his direction after I mentioned that I'd like to go back to night school to study something new. And I'm so glad he did because Harrison's been so helpful, giving me advice and course guides and talking through my options.

I've returned home feeling positive and more certain about what I want to do. I even rushed to change into pyjamas and am now curled up on the couch, looking through the guides at the many courses on offer to me.

The intercom buzzes and I check the time. It's past midnight. I answer, but no one's there. This often happens late at night when partygoers press all the buttons as they make their drunken way home. I'm about to pull the safety lock on my door, just in case, when it swings open, taking me by surprise. I step back, hitting the wall. Tanner stands before me, his shoulders squared and his nostrils flaring.

We stare at each for a few silent seconds, and then he grips a hand in my hair and tugs me to him. I crash against his hard chest, almost knocking the breath from my body. His eyes flit from my lips to my eyes, like he's struggling to come to a decision, and then he places a soft kiss on my lips.

But I can't do this if he's going to be gentle. It has to be rough, and so I push my tongue into his mouth and grip his face, my fingers digging into his skin slightly. There's no question of me turning him away. I haven't had sex since we split, and I love the sexy vibes he gives off when he's all alpha like this. Right now, I could orgasm from the way he's responding to my forceful kiss.

He begins to pull at my top, fumbling with the buttons. I use my foot to kick the door closed and then I shove him hard. He stumbles back, hitting the door, and I pounce at him, taking him by surprise. He catches me, and I wrap my legs around his waist, rubbing myself shamelessly against his erection. There's no option for him to leave me again without fucking me, and I need to make it impossible for him to say no, a second time.

"Wait, wait, wait," he pants, untangling himself from me and lowering my feet to the ground. "I need something from you first."

"This changes nothing between us, it's just sex," I point out.

He frowns. "I need you to . . ." He pauses and then grimaces. "I'm just gonna say it cos there ain't no nice way to ask. I need you to suck my cock."

I can't hide my surprise at his words, not just because they're blunt or crude, but he's never asked before. "You hate that. You've never let me do it."

"I know, that's why I need you to try. I'm working something out, and I don't trust anyone else. I know you'll stop if I ask."

I suddenly feel nervous. This was always a huge deal in our relationship. Tanner hadn't ever gone into great detail, but I knew that oral sex took him somewhere dark, so I never pushed the issue. Whenever it came up, he would just tell me that it was in his past and talking about it wouldn't help.

"Okay," I say, and relief floods his face.

"Right, okay," he puffs out, unfastening his belt. "Erm, I . . ." He pauses, looking down at his flaccid cock. This was always half the problem—whenever the thought came to him, he'd lose his erection.

"Let's go into my room, relax, and take your mind off it."

Tanner nods and follows me through to my bedroom. It feels weird now, too forced, and doubts are beginning to creep in. It's why I wanted to keep it fast and rough, but his question has changed the whole dynamic of what we were about to do. I'm overthinking. I haven't even talked to him about our divorce yet, since I've been waiting for a good time.

I begin removing pillows and adjusting the blankets nervously. "Stop that." He sighs, stilling my hands. "You're making me rethink this."

"Sorry, it feels weird now."

"It's not weird, we're married. It's just sex between two people who loved each other and aren't ready to go elsewhere." His words slay me while also bringing me relief. His use of the past tense, loved, kills my heart all over again, but the news he hasn't had sex elsewhere, including with Melissa, brings me comfort.

He leans in to kiss me again. This time, I let him lead, noticing how he's a little rougher than before. He pushes me down onto the bed and grips my knee, bending it slightly and wrapping it around his waist. He tugs down the cup of my white lace bra and flicks his tongue over my erect nipple. "I miss these." He groans, gently biting into my breast, and I arch my back. "You want it rough?" he asks, smirking. I bite his lower lip as his mouth brushes against mine, and he hisses and smiles. "Okay, you asked for it."

In one swift move, he spins me onto my front and slaps me hard on the arse. I hold onto a pillow, pushing my face into it to muffle my cries as he brings down a few more blows.

He feels around to the front of my pyjama bottoms and pulls the tie open. Tugging hard, he has them down my legs in seconds and is lining himself up at my entrance. "You know how good your arse looks when it's red like this," he whispers. His cock slams into me, pushing me up the mattress. "This is where I belong," he mumbles into my hair.

"Pity you didn't remember that six months ago," I reply dryly.

"Baby, don't start pissing me off when I have you like this," he growls, and I smirk to myself. It's how I like him, angry and hard.

"Is she in your bed, Tanner? Does she fuck you like I did?"

"She was never in my bed," he pants, pulling out his full length before slamming back inside me harder. "Stop talking shit." Before I answer, his hand reaches around to cover my mouth. "No more," he hisses.

He thrusts a few more times, keeping my mouth covered, and as I begin to shudder, I graze my teeth against the palm of his hand. He laughs at my attempt to hurt him and continues to move inside me until I'm crying out with pleasure. Eventually, he lets go of my face and pulls from inside of me. "My turn," he whispers into my ear, rolling onto his back.

I kiss his neck, running my tongue across his skin, occasionally nipping. Then, I slide between his legs until my knees hit the ground and I'm at eye-level with his erection. Gripping his shaft, I move my hand a few times, watching the glistening bead of cum slip down his hardness. Tanner pushes himself up onto his elbows, watching as I move my fist back and forth. I lick away the bead of cum. Tanner flinches, and I watch his hands ball at his sides. "You want me to stop?" I ask cautiously.

"No, do it again," he growls, his voice angry.

This time, I run my tongue over the head of his cock and then close my lips around it. Tanner hisses, squeezing his eyes closed like he's in pain. I still, letting him get used to the feeling before pushing him farther into my mouth. As he hits the back of my throat, I relax, forcing myself to take him deeper.

Tanner's body is stiff and rigid, like he's suffering rather than enjoying it, and I wonder if I'm doing it right because it's my first time too. I run my nails along his thigh, letting him know it's okay, but he tenses further, and then suddenly, he shoves me away. I fall back on my arse, and Tanner stands, pulling his jeans up. "No, no," he mutters.

"Tanner, it's okay," I whisper, wiping my mouth on the back of my hand. Tanner glances at me, but his eyes aren't seeing me. He's lost somewhere else, and as he steps over me to leave, a sob leaves my throat. I hadn't even realised it was there, but it doesn't stop him like it normally would. The front door slams closed, and I curl myself into a ball, wondering what the hell I'd just agreed to and why I suddenly feel dirty.

CHAPTER SIX

Tanner

The bottle slips out of my hand, clattering onto the floor and rolling away. I turn my head to watch it, and everything seems to be moving in slow motion. After leaving Brook, I'd found myself in a twenty-four-hour shop where I bought two bottles of whiskey. I then got as far as the car park of the clubhouse before sitting around the back of the building and cracking open the first bottle. It'd gone down quickly, and the second was now in my hand to replace the empty one that was still rolling away from me. I hear heavy boots coming and then the click of a gun.

"Tanner?" It's Kain. He tucks his gun back into his waistband. "Shit, brother, I thought someone was gonna jump me. What the hell are you doing out here?"

I wave the full bottle to him and grin. "Party for one, brother," I slur.

"It's seven in the morning. Is that early or late for you?" I feel his arm go under my own, wrapping around me and hauling me onto my unsteady feet. "Let's get you inside to sleep that bad boy off," he mutters.

Inside, I fall onto the couch in the main room, relieved no one's around to see me in this state. My eyes drift closed.

"You're a lying little shit," my father screams, his hand reaching out and pulling me towards him. "You've always been a liar. It's for attention, you selfish little prick."

"Mr. Tanner, please let go of your son." The police officer moves between us, forcing my father to release my shoulders. "Carl hasn't said anything to us. We came to you because we found some indecent photographs of him. The person involved has been arrested, but we need a statement from your son."

"Well, he isn't giving you one."

"With all due respect, that isn't just your decision. We know something has happened to your child. Don't you want the person responsible to pay for that?"

"I want you to get out of my house. Go!"

"Mr. Tanner, we're here to help." The officers are getting pissed-off. It's no good, my dad won't budge now that he's

made his mind up. The officers will leave, he'll scream at me, then he'll hit Ma and leave for a few days. That's how he works.

"Carl, do you want to talk to us about what happened?" The female officer's voice is kind and gentle.

I glance at my father, who's glaring back at me, and that expression tells me all I need to know. I look at the officer and then slowly shake my head. "Nothing happened."

"We know that isn't true because we saw the photographs. We want to help you. What if that man goes on to do things to other children?"

Emotional blackmail isn't going to work on me. No one helped me, so why should I care about what that bastard does next? When it becomes clear I'm not going to talk to them, she sighs. "Child services will be involved in this case, Mr. Tanner. They'll want to talk with Carl about what happened, and you won't have a say in that. We can't force him to talk with us, but we strongly advise that you encourage him to, because we want to see this man locked up for what he's done."

Once they leave, my dad turns on me, screaming and shouting about how I'm ruining his life. He doesn't care that his best friend has been doing things to me. All he cares about is his drinking partner might go to prison. They spend their weekends frequenting the club scene, selling drugs, drinking, and partying. He's not prepared for it to end because of me.

I later discovered that my father's friend was a big-time drug dealer and my dad owed him a lot of money. Once he was sent to prison, the next man in line took over and Dad had to find a way to pay that guy. The debt doubled when he couldn't make payments. It caused him all kinds of drama that would span into almost ten years of him ducking and diving and trying to pay back a debt that always seemed to be doubling whenever the gang leader felt like it. I used my payout from the Armed Forces to pay off the debt, not that I got any thanks for it because, according to my dad, it was all my fault anyway.

I stretch out my limbs, blinking my eyes a few times to adjust to the light streaming into the clubhouse. Sleeping on this couch has given me a backache. The club's busier now, and checking my watch, I realise it's noon. Thoughts of last night come flooding back to me and I cringe. What kind of man runs out on a woman like that? I shake my head and the room spins.

"Finally back with us?" Melissa lowers into a chair nearby. "You need to sort yourself out, Tanner. Seriously, you're going to be a father soon."

"Fuck off, Melissa. I'm not in the mood. Go clean something." I say it because it never fails to piss her off, and I need someone to feel as shitty as I do right now.

"Actually, I need some more cash. I'm going to look at an apartment today, and if I take it, I'll need the first month's rent upfront."

I like the thought of having Melissa away from the club, so I nod. "How much?"

"Let's say five grand?"

I roll my eyes and laugh. "Five grand for a month's deposit? You're setting your standards too high."

"Well, obviously, I'll need furniture for the baby and stuff."

"I've just opened my eyes. Give me a break. We'll talk about this later."

"You say that every time, Tanner. Why are you holding out on me all the time? Brook has gone, I'm here, and I want you to be in this baby's life. I don't get why you're making this so hard for yourself."

"Has anyone ever told you that you're a real nag?" I mutter, pulling myself to my feet.

"Well, I'm sick of being treated like a whore by everyone here. I deserve some damn respect. Trust me to get pregnant by a lower ranked member."

"Careful, Melissa. You're starting to sound like you did all this on purpose." I scowl at her, and she gives me a smug look.

"So, can I get some cash?" she asks.

"You can get a grand," I say, and she mumbles something about me being a tight arse. I open my wallet and pull out five hundred. "I'll get you the rest when I've had my coffee." I don't use banks, and my cash is kept under lock and key in the clubhouse.

I watch Ma chatting with Sam for the last hour, and I'd forgotten what it was like to see her smile and laugh. As I head over, she turns to me. She's already looking years lighter and she's only been away from my dad for one night. "Sam's been filling me in on life around here." She smiles.

"Yeah? He tell you he's married?" I ask, and Sam laughs. His wife died many years ago, but he's remained single ever since. Whenever we try to get him to move on, he tells us that just because his wife is dead, don't mean he ain't still married.

Ma blushes. "Oh Carl, he's just being friendly."

"He's a biker. We don't do friendly," I point out, and she taps my arm playfully. "What happens now, Ma? You wanna start fresh or go back home?"

"Start fresh? What do you mean?" she asks.

"I mean, you leave that rundown house you call a home. I can get you a new place, or you can come and stay here with me."

"Oh, I don't think I can do that. You have your own life to sort out. I'll be fine where I am."

"It's your choice, Ma, but I think it'll do Dad good to know he can't just come home when he changes his mind. You deserve better, and a fresh start will put you on the right path."

She twists her wedding ring. "I should have kicked him out a long time ago. When all that business happened, I got the life I deserved."

"Ma," I groan, taking her hands and holding them in my own, "don't talk like that. Back then, he wouldn't have let you leave. Not alive, anyway. You supported me the best you could, and I won't ever forget that." From the day the social worker left my house, my mum changed. She became more suspicious and watchful, and if Dad had any friends over, she wouldn't leave my side. Soon after everything came out, I went off the rails. I caused her so much pain, but she never blamed me. She would still tell me she loved me, even when I brought the police to her door over and over.

Brook

"I thought that you would be the hero, come and save the day, but you're a villain, your sins unforgiven . . ." I wail into the hairbrush. Singing is my new therapy. *"I catch your scent in every wind, and I recall the love we had, I can't pretend, that I don't miss you every now and then, but the hurt is for the better, moving on, it's now or never—"*

The intercom buzzes and I drop the hairbrush and reach for it. "Come in," I slur, picking up the bottle of wine and taking a large gulp. I sway towards the front door, unlatching it and leaving it open. I'd contemplated calling Mila and Harper, but I knew they'd judge my bad decisions, so I called Henry.

"I knew as soon as you texted me this morning to say you were too sick to come into work that something was wrong," he says as he comes through the door. He pauses when he sees me dancing around the living room in my underwear and one of Tanner's old shirts, the bottle dangling from my hand. "Oh lord, things are worse than I first thought," he mutters, pulling off his jacket and throwing it over the couch.

"So, I slept with Tanner," I announce, throwing my arms out like I'm on stage performing, "and then he ran out on me."

Henry sighs. "Oh sweetie."

"No," I hiss, pointing my finger at him. "Don't do that pity thing. I know I look pathetic right now, but I'm okay. I called you because I know you'll tell me like it is. You don't do pity, remember?"

He raises a questioning eyebrow. "You know what you need," he says, heading towards my kitchen and returning with a large glass of water. He holds it out for me.

"I need wine, not water," I say with despair, but I take the glass anyway and glug it down.

"I wasn't talking about the water. You need a night in a sad bar, with unappealing men, a karaoke, and shots."

"Do you think?" I sniffle. "I'm a mess."

"Exactly. I can't take you into town looking like you do. I have a reputation to uphold. But I know a great little bar that no one our age goes in. Unappealing men wall to wall."

"Why do they need to be unappealing?"

"So that you don't end up with a pity fuck. Men would smell your desperation from a mile off. We need old men who have no teeth, so you can't be tempted into making any more terrible mistake."

Henry drags me to my bedroom and pulls open the wardrobe. "I'll find your clothes. You wipe your snotty face, you're a mess." I sit in front of my mirror and take in my puffy, red, bloodshot eyes. Grabbing a wipe, I scrub off last night's makeup, paying close attention to the black smudges that have formed underneath my eyes. "That isn't any better. Get lots of concealer on," Henry says from behind me.

"Yah know, H, you're not making me feel any better," I mutter, searching through my makeup bag.

"Like you just said, I don't do pity, sweet pea. I do drinking and dancing. That makes everything better," he says with a smile. "I've texted the guys, so everyone's meeting us there."

I'd left the team in the lurch today, but there was no way I could go into work, so I'd texted to say I was ill. Of course, Henry hadn't fallen for it. He'd texted back with LIAR, assuming I was hungover.

Henry takes the lead, gripping my hand as we enter the bar. This was the same bar I'd come to meet Harrison. "I know this place," I say. It's just as quiet, with four older men sitting at a table playing cards. The bartender, Tom, recognises me, smiling widely as I approach the bar. "Tanner's girl," he states.

"No," I say a little too defensively. "Not anymore. Melissa is his girl these days."

"Oh, right. Sorry," he apologises.

"That name is now barred, so we must not speak it," says Henry firmly, and Tom smirks. "This girl needs a constant flow of wine and the karaoke."

"I'll turn the machine on for the karaoke right this minute, and I'll open up a bar tab for the flowing wine." Tom hands me a microphone with a sympathetic smile.

"And we must not tell you know who about any of this," I add.

Tom salutes like a soldier. "Gotcha."

James, William, and Blake enter a few minutes later, and James screws his face up. "Where are we?" He sounds disgusted.

"We are in heartbreak hotel. Brook is going to cry, drink, dance, and sing, and then tomorrow, she'll be better, her heart will hurt less, and she'll be the strong, independent woman we all know and love," Henry announces.

"Sounds like fun." Blake grins. "Show me the wine."

Almost an hour and four songs later, and one full bottle of wine to myself, I'm feeling no better, and I'm starting to wish I'd stayed home so there were no witnesses to my shameful heartbreak. I don't understand. I did all this six months ago when we first split up, and now, I'm here again. And what did he actually do this time apart from walk out? It's hardly a crime, yet it hurt just as much. Maybe I'm ashamed of myself for giving in yet again. Or maybe it's because I laid awake for hours after he left, overthinking. Did he feel guilty on Melissa and so he'd come to his senses and ran back to her? Did she know his history? Did he confide in the mother of his child? A pained sob escapes and I throw back another shot.

Blake grabs my hand, interrupting my racing thoughts. "I've found the perfect song," she says, grinning.

I love these guys. They took me in and made me part of their group with no questions, and now, they're rallying around to help me fix my broken heart. But I miss the MC and how my life was before all of this, back when my only concern was keeping Tanner happy.

The music begins and I laugh out loud. *"This is a shout out to my ex. Heard he in love with some other chick. Yeah, yeah, that hurt me I'll admit. Forget that boy, I'm over it."* We burst into a fit of giggles. *"I hope she gettin' better sex. Hope she ain't fakin' it like I did."* We laugh again and then begin jumping around and singing out of tune. I'm so busy laughing and yelling the words, I don't notice the door swing open. Three guys enter, and as I spin back around, I stumble. I recognise the guys from another MC.

It's a new club that set up around a year ago. I remember because they came to Cooper and asked for permission to start up their charter two counties over from the Hammers. Cooper had granted permission providing they pay a tariff. They agreed and pay on time each month, and they haven't been trouble.

All three are nice-looking, and Blake practically swoons off the stage as the song ends. I'm a little more reserved as they eye us. I haven't heard anything bad about them, but I haven't heard good either.

Approaching the bar, I notice the nearest one has the VP patch. His emblem reads 'Devil Dogs MC'.

"Who was the fucker that broke your heart, baby?" His voice is low, rumbling through me.

"I don't know what you mean," I mutter. "Same again please, Tom."

"I'll get this one, Tom," he says firmly.

"No, it's fine, thank you. Besides, we have a tab open."

"Are you gonna tell me who the stupid fucker was? I can have his legs broken, or worse, whichever suits."

"It's fine. I'm fine. Thanks." I take the glass of wine and head for the table where the others are staring open-mouthed.

"H.O.T," says Blake, sighing.

I smirk. "T.R.O.U.B.L.E."

"You know what they say, though. To get over someone—" starts James.

"Please don't finish that sentence," I cut in. "Bartender Tom knows Tanner. He'll call him and then all kinds of problems will start."

"Why? You don't belong to Tanner anymore," argues James.

"It doesn't work like that. Especially while I still have this," I say, pulling my shirt open slightly to reveal Tanner's tag on my collar bone. "The club would see it as betrayal."

"Are you shitting me? After the biggest betrayal of all?" asks Will.

"Well, I'm not attached to anyone in the Hammers, so . . ." Blake rises to her feet and heads over to the men.

"She's got some balls under that little voice and giggly persona," says Will, watching her with admiration.

CHAPTER SEVEN

Tanner

I stare into the eyes of my opponent right before smashing my fist hard into his face. I'd received a text message seconds before I was about to go in the ring from Tom, telling me that my Brook is in the same bar as some of the Devil Dogs MC guys, and my rage is out of control just thinking about them chatting to her.

After I ran out on her yesterday, I'd guessed I wasn't her favourite person, so I've come to fight rather than stalk her. And part of me knows that when I go back to see her, she's gonna want answers and I'm not sure I'm ready to give them. It isn't that I can't talk about it, I can, but I don't want to. It's my past and I've moved on . . . well, almost.

I'm so lost in thought, the punch from my opponent takes me by surprise and I hit the deck, the back of my head taking the full force. He doesn't waste time, and now he finally has me down, he lays into me, punch after punch pummelling my face. There's no ref in this match. It's underground and worth a lot of cash, and it won't stop until one of us is knocked out fully. I picture Brook getting naked with Capone, the Devil Dogs President, or worst still, Hawk, their VP. He's a known womaniser and a good-looking motherfucker. Women fall at his feet.

I growl and bring my head up, crashing it against my opponent. His skin splits immediately, and his blood washes over me. I throw him and scramble to my knees. When I glance over, he's flat on his back with his arms spread out around him. Thank fuck. The crowd is going wild, but I don't have the time or energy to celebrate.

I shower in the dull change rooms, watching the blood run down my body. All I can think about is Brook. I need to be near her, and the urge to run to her now is overwhelming. "Tanner, you in here still?" Cooper's voice brings me from my Brook daydream.

"Yeah," I mutter, and I hear his steps get closer.

"What happened back there? You got hit." He sounds shocked because it doesn't happen often.

"I like to put on a show," I lie. "The crowd loves it."

"I'm not complaining. You made me a tidy sum out there tonight. You've got some interest, too. A few guys wanna fight you next."

"Set it up." I sigh, turning off the water and grabbing my towel.

"You don't wanna discuss it with them?"

"No, I don't have time. Give me a week to heal properly and then arrange the next one."

"You don't have time? What's going on with you lately?"

"My dad's left my ma. I have shit going on, Coop." I'm tired of him always asking what I'm doing or where I'm at, like he's my damn keeper.

"I know that, brother. You need help with any of it? Cos we're here for you, man," he offers.

I pull on my clothes. "Thanks, Pres, I'm all good. I need to track down my dad, now Mum's not on his radar, I need to settle a score."

"A *final* settlement?" asks Cooper, raising a brow.

I shrug my shoulders. "It depends how it goes down. I'm not planning on it, but never say never. I'll keep the club out of it, don't worry."

"Tanner, I'm not worried about the club, I'm worried about you. You keep going off radar, you're turning up drunk in the mornings, you're stalking Brook, and you've moved Melissa into the club. You have a lot going on and you're not talking to any of us. You're not on your own, brother."

I appreciate the speech, and I know my brothers would be at my side if I need them, but involving them means explaining, and I don't want to go over that shit about why my dad hates me, how he blames me for losing his best friend and getting into debt, or how he detests me because I'm living the life that he wanted. "I know, brother. I got this text before I went in the ring," I say, holding out my phone. "I lost my mind for a second, but I'm okay." I'm hoping at least half an explanation for me taking that beating will be enough to get him off my back.

"Brook wouldn't go there, brother, out of respect for you and the club."

"I wouldn't blame her if she did, Coop. I'd deserve it. I wouldn't like it, but I'd deserve it."

"What's the plan? We go storming in and start a war with the Devils?"

I don't miss the way he says 'we'. He's telling me he's got my back on this. "Maybe we should show our faces, so they know we know her, but I don't plan on starting any trouble. It'll only push Brook towards them. You know how stubborn she is."

"Good point. Okay, I'll get Kain, and we'll meet you out front."

I watch Cooper go and sigh. I should walk away. Brook won't appreciate me storming in there, but I can't just sit back and let her think I'm giving up.

Brook

I lie still and keep my arms pressed tight into my sides. I press my lips together so that I don't laugh again. The VP of the Devil Dogs is carefully balancing our shot glasses on my stomach. "Okay, roll the dice," he finally shouts.

Blake rolls the dice. "Two," she announces, "And I choose . . ." She looks around at everyone and then points to Hawk, who groans dramatically. He's already been chosen three times. He smirks at me, jumping on the bar and positioning himself with his crotch over my face. He's trying to make me spill the shots by being provocative, and each time he's gotten a little braver. He places his hands behind his back and leans over to my stomach to take a shot glass in his mouth. He throws his head back and necks the shot like an expert before moving along and doing it a second time.

Somehow, it went from Blake chatting with Breaker, the Devil Dogs Enforcer, to us doing body shots. But I have to admit, they seem like nice guys so far, and we've done nothing but laugh. Plus, it's taken my mind off everything else.

Hawk peers at me through his legs. "Spillage," he says with a grin, and then he proceeds to lean over and run his tongue across my abdomen. I squeeze my eyes shut again, trying not to laugh at the sensation of his warm tongue tickling my side. The rules were that if I laughed and spilt any of the shots, I'd have to drink the rest.

Suddenly, the door opens, letting in a cool breeze, and my eyes fix on Cooper as his large body fills the doorway. He steps inside, followed by Kain and then Tanner. Hawk wipes his mouth before jumping down off the bar. "Cooper, great to see you, brother." He holds out his hand, and Cooper shakes it. I lie still, hoping they won't spot me. "You wanna come play body shots?" asks Hawk, moving to one side to reveal me. I turn my head away.

"I will," says Tanner, and I know instantly he's spotted me.

"Actually, I'm done," I announce.

"You're done when I say," snaps Tanner, stepping closer and glaring down at me. "Roll the dice," he orders. Blake looks at me for confirmation. I take in Tanner's bruised face. He's not going to let me up without causing a drama, so I nod to her to go ahead.

Blake rolls. "One," she mutters. The place has fallen eerily silent, and I notice Cooper is quietly talking to Hawk in the far corner.

"My lucky number," whispers Tanner, leaning over me. He takes the shot in his mouth, his beard grazing over my skin and causing me to shiver. He knocks the shot back and places the glass on the bar. "Mmm, sambuca . . . remember when you'd lay naked and let me lick it from you?"

I begin to remove the last three shot glasses from my body and sit up. Tanner steps in front of me, placing his hands either side of my legs. At this height, I'm able to stare directly into his eyes, and they're wild. I feel the energy swirling between us. "Move," I growl.

"Make me," he hisses.

"Why are you here?"

"I came to tell you," he murmurs close to my ear, glancing to where Cooper and Hawk are still talking, "that if you so much as kiss one of these men, that's us done. I won't follow you. I won't turn up at your apartment. We will be over. There'll be no going back from that."

My blood boils. After everything he's done, he has the audacity to stand before me and spout this bullshit. "How the fuck dare you?" I hiss, my voice low and menacing.

"It'll cause a war, Brook, you know that. I won't be able to just turn my back. It'll be a direct disrespect to me and the club. You're my ol' lady, and I'd have to kick his arse and cut you from my life and the club's."

"Like you've already done," I snap.

"It was your choice to walk out on the club, and you know they'd take you back anytime."

I take a calming breath. "I was just having a few drinks with my friends. Hawk felt sorry for me and was helping to cheer me up." I push myself down from the bar, and Tanner steps back. "But now you've set me a challenge," I say, adding a smile.

Realising his mistake, he groans. "Brook," he says, his tone warning, "I'm serious about this."

I guess he underestimates how much I need him to leave me alone and stop following me. I'll never get over him if he carries on being around, and so I saunter over to where Cooper and Hawk are talking. Stepping between the two, I glance back to where Tanner is rooted to the spot, his eyes wild and his fists scrunched tightly.

"I'm really sorry for doing this," I say, turning back to face Hawk, "but you know how you said you'd help to mend my broken heart?" Hawk nods, his eyes narrowing when I indicate for him to lower his ear so I can whisper something. When his face is close enough, I lean forward and press my lips on his, taking him by surprise. I place my hands gently on his face and proceed to move my mouth against his. After a few shocked seconds, he kisses me back. It feels strange. I haven't kissed anyone since Tanner, and it's completely different, soft and gentle where Tanner is rough and fiery.

The sound of breaking glass has Hawk pulling away, and then he tugs me behind him for safety.

"Don't put her behind you. It isn't your damn job to protect her!" Tanner yells. Cooper's in front of him, trying to talk him down from his rage.

Hawk smirks. "I think you knew that would happen, firecracker. You after some trouble?"

"No," I snap, "but I won't have him telling me what I can and can't do. I'm not his ol' lady anymore."

"Looks like he thinks different," he mutters, and I step from behind Hawk. Tanner wouldn't hurt me, not even with the lost, vacant look that he currently has in his eyes. "I don't think that's a good idea," adds Hawk.

"Tanner, stop," I snap angrily.

He freezes, his chest heaving and his shoulders hunched. "Why would you do that?" he almost whispers, and the pain in his voice is raw.

"We are over. You decided that the minute you stuck your dick in Melissa. How dare you come in here with threats about us being completely done if I kiss another man? We were already done, you made sure of that. And now I've released you. You can stop following me and turning up where I am. There is nothing between us. I'm not sure there ever really was."

Tanner takes a step back, like my words have punched him in the gut. "That's not true," he mutters.

"Isn't it? We never talked. We fought, fucked, and the rest of the time, you just watched me. It's taken all of this to make me see that, and last night, you proved it. You didn't stay and talk. You walked, again, always walking away. This," I say, pointing to Hawk, "if this is what it takes to set you free," I inhale a shaky breath, tears beginning to fill my eyes, "well then, now you're free. We both are." I snatch my clutch bag from the table and walk out of the bar, leaving the place in silence.

I'm almost home when a cab pulls up alongside me. "Wait for us, honey," shouts James from the open window. They all dive out, and I'm wrapped in hugs, then we walk with our arms linked back to my place.

Once inside, I lock the door and use the safety chain. I'm not sure if Tanner really means what he said or if he'll turn up in a rage. Whenever we had big arguments at the clubhouse, he'd put his fists through the drywall or a door, mainly because he hated being away from me and he knew that if I was mad, I'd hide away from him for a day or so.

"I can't believe what happened back there," Blake says.

"I need a tattoo removed or covered. Any of you know someone who can help me with that?" I ask. To make it all final, I'll need to cover his name on my skin. It would be the final blow—that and the divorce papers, which I still haven't presented Tanner with—and equally as important to the club.

"We'll find somebody on Monday. Sleep on it. You've had a lot to drink, and things have come to an emotional head, so get some sleep," says Will.

"Oh please," tuts Henry, "I think she made herself pretty clear tonight, and I think it's the right decision. Fuck him. You can do so much better, Brook."

I smile. "Thanks Henry. And thanks for tonight. You guys really helped to cheer me up. Without that, I doubt I would have stood up to him like I did."

"Well, here's to the future." James smiles, kissing me on the cheek. "Now, let's get some sleep. I'm exhausted after all the drama."

Tanner

Cooper and Kain drive me from Tom's bar to a lookout point a few miles out of town. We share a bottle of whiskey and wait for the sun to rise. It's been a long time since we've done this.

"What was she talking about when she said you ran out on her last night?" asks Kain.

"Just that. We hooked up," I say, swigging from the bottle and passing it to Cooper.

"Do you think there's hope for you guys? I mean, if she's letting you back to hook up—"

I laugh, shaking my head. "Nah, man, not now. I've done too much. I'm done. I'm gonna get on top of every fucking woman in town until I forget all about Brook."

"Wow, big statement seeing as you've spent the last, what, ten years following her around."

"Yeah, well, I thought she was the one. Turns out I was wrong."

"Whatever, man. You were meant to be and you still are. So, you fucked up, we all do that sometimes. Look how badly Cooper and I fucked shit up, and we still won our women back."

I smile at the memory of the dramas we've endured as a club. I pick up a stick and began to dig a hole in the dirt. "Do you remember my old man?"

"How could we forget that piece of shit?" growls Cooper.

"He blames me for some shit that happened when I was a kid. He wants blood and told my mum that he's getting payback."

"What kind of shit would make him so bitter that he'd still be coming for you years later?"

I take a deep breath. I didn't plan to tell the guys about my childhood, but there's something freeing about being up here with them after the night I've had. I want a fresh start, so I need to be honest. And Brooks was right, I'm always running away. "He had a friend, someone who was always around. We called him Kenny. Anyway, he's in jail now, I think. He was only sentenced to five years, but he couldn't behave in there and kept getting time added on. The last time I checked, he was still inside." I'm rambling through my nerves, but the guys sit quietly, waiting for me to finish. "I check regular, not because I care, but because when I finally get my chance, I'm going to slit his throat."

"What's he in jail for, Tanner?" asks Cooper.

"Assault on a child, sexual," I mutter, keeping my eyes downcast. Suddenly, I feel like a child again, sitting with all those important people while they dissected what happened. Because despite my father trying to shut it down, the Crown Prosecution charged Kenny and the whole case went to trial. I didn't have to give evidence because he pleaded guilty. "On me... sexual assault on me," I clarify. "He got five years in jail. It wasn't sex, it was other stuff." It feels good to finally say it, and when I look up, my brothers are staring straight ahead, lost in thought.

"Shit, brother, I would never have guessed," mutters Cooper.

"Yeah, well, they don't give you a badge or anything," I say, trying to lighten the mood. "I was a kid, eleven or something like that. Turned out there were other kids too, not just me, but for some reason, they only had evidence on me, photographs and shit."

"That fucker should be in the ground," growls Kain. "When he gets out, we'll be waiting for him."

I smile. They aren't judging me, and they have my back. "The thing is, Melissa said something the other night. That's what spiralled this whole thing in the first place. She said she'd sucked my cock. Well, she couldn't have because I can't do that. I can't let anyone do that." I pause, letting that sink in. "And so last night, I tried it with Brook. I trust her, and I wondered if things had changed, if I'd let Mel do it because I felt different now. Anyway, turns out I still can't stand it. It takes me straight back to that dark room and," I pause, biting my inner cheek, "I ran out on Brook. She doesn't know about all that stuff."

"What are you saying, Tanner?" asks Cooper.

"I'm saying maybe Melissa is lying."

"About having sex with you or just sucking your cock?" Kain asks.

"I'm not sure. Maybe she was just shooting her mouth off, but something feels off about the whole thing. With that and my dad doing a disappearing act, I just have a bad feeling. I can't rule out that this is some big payback plot."

"Payback for what, man? You were a kid," says Cooper.

"Yeah, he doesn't see it that way. I might be overthinking the whole thing, but I need to be on my guard."

"And if you're right," begins Kain.

"Then I didn't cheat on my wife."

CHAPTER EIGHT

Brook

The days have blurred into one and it's been a whole week since the whole Tanner incident in the bar. We've been so busy at the salon that I haven't had any time to wallow in self-pity. I've made sure to spend the evenings just as busy. I joined a gym, went swimming, and I ate out with either Blake or Henry. Tanner isn't around. I haven't felt him all week, and he hasn't bothered to text or check up on me. I know it's what I wanted and I should feel happy, but inside I feel empty. Every little hurdle feels like the very first time he broke my heart, and the pain just seems to go on and on.

I decided to keep Friday night free so I could trawl the internet for career ideas, but as I sit in front of my laptop, my intercom buzzes. I'm surprised to hear Cooper's voice. "Brook, can I come up?"

I let him in, and he follows me to the kitchen. "I didn't expect you. What's up?"

"I'm having to put the club on lockdown," he states, folding his large arms over his wide chest.

"Okay, and you're telling me because . . ." I wait for him to finish my sentence.

"You know how this works, Brook. You need to come with me."

I shake my head, laughing nervously. "No, I'm nothing to do with the club these days."

"I know, but unfortunately, you're still seen as part of us. The threat is towards Tanner, which means you could be at risk. His dad is causing all kinds of problems, and as a precaution, I'd like you to stay at the club."

"No," I say firmly. "There's no way I can stay at the clubhouse after everything that's happened. I have a job and responsibilities that don't just stop because you decide that you want a lockdown."

"Brook, you know I wouldn't take the decision lightly. If I'm putting us on lockdown, then there's a real threat. Until I can locate Tanner's dad, you aren't safe. If you don't come with me willingly, I'll take you out of here kicking and screaming," he says firmly.

I know it's not an empty threat. He'd take me out of here against my will and not give a shit who sees. "For how long?" I ask on a sigh.

"Hopefully, no longer than the weekend. I've spoken to your boss, and he was fine about you taking tomorrow. I promised I'd have you at work Monday, but if I haven't found Tanner's dad, then I'll personally escort you there myself and keep watch."

"For goodness sake, I thought I'd left all this behind," I complain. "Will I ever be rid of that man?"

Half an hour later, I find myself entering the clubhouse. After not being here for months, it feels like my worlds are colliding, past and present crashing together, and I hate it. I hate that I instantly feel like an outsider, even though I spent years living here. Woody is the first to spot me, and he jumps from his chair and rushes over, sweeping me into a bear hug and swinging me around. The problem with my petite size is that all these huge men automatically lift me up. I can't deny I've missed it.

"Baby girl, you're home." He grins, lowering me to the ground.

"Not for long, Woody. Just a short stay to make your Pres happy."

"Oh," he says, glancing at Cooper. "What's going on?"

"Lockdown. Spread the word," mutters Cooper.

"Since when?" Woody asks, clearly confused.

"Since now. Spread the damn word!"

Kurt and Shane come barrelling through the doors laughing and they stop at the sight of me. "Mama's back," declares Shane, grinning. Both prospects are of similar age to me, but they've always referred to me as Mama Bear.

"I hope you've been keeping out of trouble." They both laugh, looking guilty as hell. A squeal gets my attention and I smile when I spot Mila running my way.

"You got her to come," she says, winking at Cooper.

He kisses her on the forehead. "I promised you Brook, and here she is." Mila takes my hand and pulls me through the clubhouse until we reach Harper and Kain's bedroom. She knocks once on the door and then opens it. Harper is laying on her bed.

She grins when she sees me. "You came! We thought you wouldn't."

I shrug, stepping towards the bed and setting my bag on the ground. "I guess I was tempted to see everyone. It was a good excuse to come."

"Well, Tanner is supposed to be on a long run, so hopefully, you won't bump into him, and we haven't seen much of Melissa."

"I'm not bothered about seeing her. She should be more worried about seeing me," I state, and Harper laughs. Not that I would do anything bad to her since she's pregnant. If she'd slept with Tanner without knowing about me, perhaps I wouldn't feel so much hatred towards her, but she knew. I'd been around for years, and everyone in the club knew I was Tanner's ol' lady.

"I also need your help. I'd like to get Tanner's name covered. I'd booked into a tattooist in town for tomorrow, but now we're stuck here..."

"We'll get Tatts to do it. While we're on lockdown, he won't have anything better to do. Besides, he'll spend the weekend tattooing the guys," says Mila, and I nod. They're the words I wanted to hear, though I'm not sure Tatts will do it just on my say so. He'll need to check with Tanner or someone of higher ranking. As if reading my mind, Mila adds, "Don't worry, I'll get Cooper to ask him."

By the evening, the club's packed out. All the guys have brought their families, so there're ol' ladies and kids everywhere. As usual when lockdowns happen, the guys all sit at one end of the clubhouse drinking bourbon and catching up, while the women sit at the other end with bottles of wine and sharing stories about their kids or their men. I've always loved lockdowns. It's the one time everyone is together, no excuses. But this time, it feels wrong, like I'm an imposter. Melissa is hanging around the place, but she's avoiding me, which suits me just fine. Every so often, I catch her looking over at me with the other ol' ladies, her hand resting on her rounded stomach with a look of anger on her face. I understand why she hates me right now—she's stepped into my life, but the ol' ladies still flock to me, and it pisses her off because she wants their respect as Tanner's new woman.

The following day, I sit back in the reclining chair as Tatts brushes his finger over my tattoo. "You're definitely sure about this? I don't want Tann coming in here beating my ass."

Mila sighs. "Will you just relax, Tatts. She's not with him anymore. Cooper's okayed this."

Tatts takes a deep breath. "Fine, okay." He rubs cleaning fluid over my old tattoo and begins drawing with pen onto my skin. "We're going for roses, right?" he confirms, and I nod, nerves making me feel nauseous.

After five minutes of Tatts drawing, he sits back. "Okay, have a look at that and see if you're happy." He holds up a small mirror, and I smile at his artwork.

"Perfect," I confirm. "I love it."

"Then let's do this." Tatts grins, starting up his machine.

We're ten minutes in when the door opens and Mila's eyes widen, I know just by the look on her face that it's Tanner. "Shit, what the hell is he doing here? He's supposed to be gone for a few days," she mutters.

"Oh fantastic, just what I need," I huff. "Tell me if he comes over."

"Shit, he's coming, he's coming," she whispers with panic in her voice. Her eyes are darting all over, completely giving the game away.

Tanner's shadow falls over us. Tatts looks up and gives a nervous smile. "Hey, brother," he greets.

"What's this?" asks Tanner.

"A tattoo," mutters Mila, rolling her eyes.

"You're just gonna come in my club and disrespect me like this?" he asks me, his voice cold. I've only ever witnessed this tone when he's being intimidating to another man. He's certainly never used it towards me.

"Sorry, I thought you were out for a few days. I was booked to have it done at a tattoo shop, but then Cooper dragged me here and so . . ." I'm trying to explain to keep him calm, but half of me wants to tell him to fuck off because it isn't his business anymore.

"Fine, if that's how you wanna be, Tatts you can do my cover-up next?" He sits on the seat nearby, putting his boots up on the table and folding his arms across his chest. I roll my eyes at his attempt to hurt me back. I don't care if he gets my name covered, it's only fair, but he's acting childish and it pisses me off.

"Sure, big man, any idea what you want?"

"Maybe you could have Melissa's name?" quips Mila, and I wince at her boldness.

"Maybe." Tanner shrugs, and I grip the sides of the chair, knowing he's just reacting to what Mila said, but I don't want to be a part of this conversation. "I just want it blacked out," he adds.

"You sure? It's a big tattoo," says Tatts. My name is written in big, bold letters down Tanner's arm. "We could do a nice design, maybe even turn it into part of your sleeve?"

"No, nothing can go there now. Just black it out." My heart squeezes, and things feel like they're snowballing. Doubts begin to creep in. Removing the tattoo is final, and it was such a big thing for Tanner when I first had it done.

I'm so lost in thought that I don't hear the ink gun stop buzzing. "All done." Tatts wipes over the new ink. He passes me a mirror, and I look at the rose that now covers where Tanner's name once was.

"Wow, it's so pretty." Mila smiles. It is really pretty, the detail's amazing, but I feel sad. I've made another step towards the freedom I never wanted, and with Tanner right beside me watching, it feels so much worse.

Tanner
I scowled at every stroke of the needle as it wiped more of me from her life. The need to smash shit up is overwhelming as I watch Brook's face while she examines her new ink. I know she regrets it, or at least feels sad about it, because it's written all over her face. She loved having my name on her skin, just like I loved having hers.

Cooper pops his head out from his office. "Tanner, you're back early. Did it go okay?"

I nod. He knew I'd rush back once he told me Brook was here. I'm still unsure as to why he called lockdown, but I can't talk right now, I'm too pissed-off.

Tatts' hand shifts slightly as he cleans up Brook's ink. He almost touches her breast, and I stand abruptly, getting everyone's attention.

"Baby, you're back." Melissa's voice breaks the awkward silence, and she bounds over, kissing me on the cheek. She's never done it before, so I know it's a show for Brook. I place my hand on her lower back, and she smiles up at me. "Let's go talk upstairs," she says, adding a wink. I let her lead me from the room knowing it'll hurt Brook further, but I'm being a prick over the tattoo incident. It's how I deal.

As soon as we're out of sight, I remove my hand from her. "I saw you were struggling back there," she says, "so thought I'd get you out before," she shrugs, "yah know, before your head exploded or something. You're welcome," she adds dryly.

"How's the house hunting going?"

"I think I have a place, if you can help me each month with the rent."

"I'll do what I can," I mutter.

"There is another way," she says with a smile. "You could just pay me one lump sum of cash."

"What the hell are you talking about?"

"I can disappear from your life. I know you love Brook, and with me and this baby out of the picture, you could win her back."

I stare at her for a second, allowing her words to sink in. "Let me get this straight. You want a lump sum of money to leave, take the kid and go?" I clarify, and she nods. Does she seriously think I'm that stupid? "And what happens when the cash runs out? You turn up and hit me up for more?"

"No, we can sign something if it makes you happy. Say . . ." She pauses and makes a show of thinking. "Two hundred and fifty thousand pounds?"

I almost choke on my laugh. "Are you shitting me?"

"It's expensive bringing up a child," she says defensively.

"What makes you think I have that kind of cash? I live in this dump and occasionally pull a shift at the garage." I shake my head in disbelief, wondering if this chick is slightly crazy.

"I thought you were good for the cash," she mutters.

"Yeah, well, you thought wrong." I leave her to think about that and head back to Tatts. I have a name to cover up.

I spot my mum, one of the prospects following her, carrying her overnight bag. I kiss her on the cheek. "No sign of Dad yet?" I ask, because if he'd have been back home, she wouldn't be here now. She shakes her head, but she doesn't look sad like she used to look when she thought about him.

"It's all very exciting, Carl." She smiles, looking around the crowded clubhouse.

"Um, you may not be saying that later when they're all partying until the early hours. Things can get pretty rowdy around here."

"Oh my, is that Brooky?" she asks, and before I can reply, she's heading towards Brook. I watch as they embrace. Mum touches Brook's hair like she's complementing her on it, and Brook blushes.

"Does that spell trouble?" asks Kain, nudging me with his arm.

"No, Ma loves her. I'd be more worried if she was talking to Mel. Yah know, the crazy bitch just asked me for two hundred and fifty thousand pound for her and the baby to disappear from my life."

Kain laughs. "Be cheaper to kill her and get Chopper to burn the evidence," he jokes.

"She's lost her damn mind."

Brook glances my way, it's the look she usually gives when she needs me to rescue her, and I guess my mum is asking awkward questions. "I better go over there," I mutter. Kain pats me on the back, laughing.

"Everything okay?" I ask, standing beside Mum.

"Brooky misses you, I can see it in her eyes," Mum states.

"Ma, don't do that," I groan. "We aren't together, accept it."

"No, you belong together, and I won't rest until you've sorted this mess out."

"Well, you'll be waiting a long time," I snap, and Brook raises her eyebrows in surprise. I guess my tone was a little abrupt. "I have a name to cover up, excuse me," I huff, heading over to where Tatts is. "Let's get this done."

It's almost three in the morning, and I was right about it getting crazy around here. The party's only just begun to break up. I drink my bourbon slowly, occasionally letting my eyes wander up and down Brook's petite body as she stands nearby, talking to Mila and Harper. I've endured a whole night of watching her chat with my brothers. I know they've missed her and they're all pleased to see her, but it's hard sitting back and watching her laugh and smile at them when she hates me so much. It's been so long since I've sat back like this and watched her breeze around the place like a breath of fresh air. I felt at home, relaxed and calm just because she was near.

"Man, you're doing that weird shit again." Cooper sighs, sitting beside me. "Stop staring at her, it's creepy."

"Why are we on lockdown?" I ask, not taking my eyes from her.

"Just thought it was the right thing to do. We don't know where your dad is, and he made a direct threat."

"Bullshit. You aren't scared of my dad," I mutter. "What's the real reason?"

"Remember who you're talking to," says Cooper firmly, "and don't question me."

"So, now you wanna pull rank?" I ask suspiciously. It's obvious he's hiding something.

"This is all for your own good, so don't question my decisions and just make the most of Brook being under the same roof as you," he says, adding a wink. "We've found your dad, by the way. I've put a guy on him."

I sit up straighter. "And?"

"And nothing. He's the other side of town, doesn't seem to be bothering anyone, and so far, he's alone. We haven't seen anything concerning, but we'll keep on him for another forty-eight hours. Kain wants to go after the guy who hurt you as a kid," he says, eyeing me for a reaction. I thought Kain would want revenge on my behalf, but that shit belongs to me.

"He's in prison. He's always in and out."

"We can get to him in there," says Cooper, frowning. "You know we can."

"I want him, Pres. I've waited for years, and every time he's released, he ends up back inside pretty much straight away. His life is mine to take out, but I appreciate Kain wanting to help with that."

"Just say the word if you change your mind, brother. It takes one phone call."

"You have twenty-four hours left until we take the club off lockdown. You're wasting time," says Kain. The last twenty-four hours passed in a blur of alcohol and sleep. Being around Brook and not being able to touch her is harder than I ever imagined. She's walking around the clubhouse like she's never been away. She was even nice to Melissa last night, asking about her pregnancy like she's over me, and that shit hurts.

I roll over, turning my back to Kain, who burst into my bedroom just now to try and get me out of bed, so I can follow Brook around like some loser. Kain and Cooper have been obsessed with pushing me her way. They don't get it—she isn't interested, and I don't blame her. "Get out," I grumble, pulling the sheets over my head.

"Tanner, after tomorrow, Brook will be gone, and all she's seen so far is your drunk arse. Show her how much you need her, how you've missed her. Do something to get her back," he says desperately.

"What's going on with you and Cooper trying to get us back together?" I huff.

"You belong together, man. We all know it. You're miserable without her."

I sit up, scowling at Kain. "Did you plan this?"

"What?" he asks innocently.

"This lockdown. Was this your way to get us under the same roof?"

Kain shrugs casually, and I know by the expression on his smug face that I'm right. "Jesus Christ, if she finds out, you're both dead, and I'm not saving your arses."

"Actually, it was Cooper's idea, not mine, but I happen to think it was quite clever."

"Man, you saw she got rid of the tattoo, right?" I ask, and he shrugs his shoulders again. "She watched me get rid of hers too, not an ounce of regret on her pretty little face. She's moved on. She isn't into me anymore."

"Then it's up to you to get her back. Without your mark on her, she's fair game. She's on the Devil Dogs' radar now, so Hawk will be watching for her."

The thought of her with someone like Hawk makes my blood boil. "Get the fuck out, Kain, and stop interfering."

By the time I'm fully awake and showered, it's almost lunchtime. Having all the Hammers under one roof is becoming tiresome and I can't wait for things to go back to normal. Brook passes me, her scent filling my nose, and I track her with my eyes. She looks more like the Brook I remember, her ass almost hanging out of her cut-offs, her hair flowing down her back, and a tight white vest clinging to her breasts. She suddenly stops and turns back to face me. "I need to talk to you when you have a minute," she says. It's the first time she's spoken to me since the tattoo incident.

"About?" I can't help but keep my tone cold and distant. Maybe it's a protection thing, but it just seems to come out that way, even when I don't intend it to.

"About us. Well, not us, but the next step in our . . ." She's stumbling over her words, which tells me she's nervous. "Our breakup," she adds.

"Okay, go on."

She sucks in a deep breath and then looks around. The room is busy, and she's uncomfortable. "Can we go somewhere quiet?"

I sigh heavily, like it's a big inconvenience, and then I head towards the office. Cooper is talking to some of the brothers, so I know it's free. I push the door open and wait for her to step inside before following her. "Make it quick," I snap.

"It can wait, if you're busy," she begins, and I roll my eyes, which pisses her off. She juts out her chin and clenches her fists.

"Just get on with it, Brook."

"I want a divorce," she blurts out. It catches me off guard and I glare at her for a few seconds. "It makes sense. We can't stay married."

"No," I say firmly, "not happening." I walk out of the office and I hear her footsteps following me.

"Tanner, wait, let's talk," she shouts after me, trying to keep up with me. Cooper watches me cautiously. "Tanner," cries Brook, and I turn to face her.

"The answer is no. Now, leave it," I warn her. My blood is pumping fast. I can hear the whooshing sound in my ears, and I know if I don't get out of here soon, I'm going to explode.

"Grow the fuck up," she yells, and this causes some of the other brothers to stop their conversations and turn to see what all the fuss is about. "I've got the papers here. Sign them and you can get on with your life," she adds angrily.

CHAPTER NINE

Brook

Tanner is filled with rage. I can't believe he didn't even suspect that this was coming. Did he think we'd stay married even though we're separated?

"Everything okay?" asks Cooper, approaching us. Neither of us look his way, our eyes locked, his filled with pain and mine filled with exasperation.

"Tanner, don't make this harder than it already is." I sigh. "It's the next step."

"Make it harder? Are you fucking shitting me right now?" he growls. "I've tried to give you space, I've tried to make things easier on you, and you keep pushing shit to the next level. First, you change your address, and then your job, and then your damn hair," he shouts, stepping towards me. I don't move back, standing firm and looking up at him. "You cover my mark on your skin and now you want a fucking divorce!"

"You cheated!" I finally scream. "You cheated, and whatever happened after that is inconsequential."

"I fucked up once. In our whole time together, I fucked up once. I worshipped you, but I messed up. Don't I deserve a second chance?" he yells.

"I think you should take this somewhere else," says Cooper.

"No," I snap, ignoring Cooper, "you did the one thing that I can never ever forgive you for. You denied me a child and then went and gave one to someone else. I can't ever look at you the way I used to." A strangled noise leaves my throat and I realise all too late that I'm crying. "Sign the papers, Tanner. I don't want to be your wife anymore." I turn, heading to my bedroom. A loud crashing sound makes me glance back in time to see Tanner losing his shit, knocking a table to the ground and causing all the glasses to topple and smash. It won't work. He can smash every piece of furniture in sight, but I will not back down. I'm filing for divorce.

I get to my room and gather my things together, then rush back downstairs, divorce papers in one hand and my bag in the other.

Cooper has Tanner pinned to the wall, talking quietly into his ear. Tanner's eyes find mine and they fall to the papers I have in my hand. Kain steps in front of me. "Not now, Brook. It's not the time," he says firmly.

I shove the papers into my bag. "Get him to come and sign them." And I head for the door.

"Brook, where are you going?" shouts Kain.

"I don't belong here," I say loud enough for them all to hear. "This is not my life anymore."

"Brook, stop!" Cooper shouts, but I keep walking until the fresh afternoon air hits my face. "Brook!" yells Cooper. I hear the heavy thud of his boots as he chases me down. "Brook, don't disrespect me in my own club, or I'll have to make an example," he warns me.

I spin to face him. "Good luck explaining that one to Mila," I mutter. "I'm leaving, Cooper. I can't be around Tanner for a second longer."

He sighs. "You two are meant to be, Brook. You know you are."

"We were, but not anymore. In fact, I should tell you that I plan to go on a date with Hawk."

"Come on, Brook. Of all the men in the world, you wanna go to another club?" He almost laughs like it's unbelievable. "If you do that, it's purely to piss Tanner off. You don't think he's punishing himself enough?"

I scoff. Tanner's only punishment is that his obsession with me has come to an end, and he depended on that for a long time. "Hawk's my type, so of course I'm interested in him."

"You know what, Brook, do it. If you think that'll make you happy, then go for it. I thought you were better than that. You've been like a little sister to me, to most of the men in this club, but if you go to the Devil Dogs, you'll no longer be welcome around here," he says firmly, and I nod stiffly. "And that includes my wife and kids," he adds. I take a step back, feeling like he's punched me in the gut.

"Mila would never let you stop her seeing me," I say. She's her own person and she wouldn't let Cooper boss her around or tell her who she can and can't be friends with. "And you say I'm like a sister, yet you were all so quick to lie for Tanner. You've been his support, not mine."

"It'd hurt me to cut you off, Brook. I love you like family, and this whole weekend has been about you and Tanner. I care about you both and I want the best for you, but if you go to the Devils, then Mila will no longer be a part of your life. It wouldn't be safe for her to associate with you."

"I have to choose Mila or getting on with my life?"

Cooper places his hands on his hips and looks down at the ground, choosing his words carefully. "You're making the choice to leave this club. You know that mixing with Hawk and his crew will lead to us cutting ties. It's us or them, you can't have both."

"I have to go," I mutter. It all feels too much right now, and I need space to clear my head. I hadn't given Hawk a second thought until now. He was nice, and I liked how he looked at me. It felt good, like when I first met Tanner. But being backed into a corner now made me think about him again. I don't have any intentions of seeing him, and I have no idea why I'm trying to hurt Cooper as he's been nothing but nice to me. Part of me feels abandoned by them all. They claim to be like my brothers, yet when it came down to it, they stuck by Tanner.

"Take care, Brook," he says, and then he turns his back on me and goes inside. I swipe angrily at the tears dripping down my cheeks. It all feels so final.

It's been a week since I walked away from Cooper outside the Hammers clubhouse, and since then, I haven't heard from anyone, not even Mila or Harper. That hurts my heart, and I'm starting to question whether we were ever really friends at all.

"Girl, will you please just text them?" Henry sighs. "It's bothering you, so sort it out."

"No," I reply stubbornly. "If Mila was a true friend, she would have told Cooper to fuck off."

"Would you?" asks Henry with a laugh. "Because seriously, that guy is scary. I can just imagine him angry." He shudders his shoulders dramatically.

"Aren't you worried they might come after you and kill you?" asks Blake, and we all turn to her with confusion. She stares back at us innocently. "Well, you must have seen stuff, secrets or whatever. They might kill you to keep you quiet." She shrugs.

"You've watched too many episodes of *Sons of Anarchy*." Henry laughs, shaking his head.

"I haven't seen shit. Women don't get involved in club business," I add. "Do you guys think I lived a life of murder and rock 'n roll?" I laugh.

"What if something happened to them? There might be a good reason why no one's been in touch," suggests Will thoughtfully. I'd already thought of that. When we got to mid-week and I hadn't felt Tanner watch me, and the girls hadn't been in touch to find out why I'd left the lockdown, I got worried and drove past the clubhouse. Motorcycles were lined up outside as usual, and I'd seen Tanner outside having a cigarette. And honestly, he looked good, better than I'd seen him look in weeks. He'd been with Jase, and they were laughing at something. I arrived home after that feeling deflated. I didn't want Tanner to sit around upset over me, or even following me, although I must admit I felt much safer having him around. I just wasn't expecting him to look so happy and normal. It was the hint I needed to really move on, not just put a show on for everyone watching.

Henry assumes I'm moping around because I haven't heard from the girls, when in fact, I've done something really stupid and now I feel like a fool. I messaged Hawk. He'd put his number in my mobile right before drinking shots off my body. I told him I'd never use it, but after my argument with Cooper and the MC backing off, plus hours of debating in my own head, I decided to go ahead and text him. It was just a general, *'hey, how are yah doing'* kind of text, but he hasn't replied, so now, I feel two things—stupid because he's ghosted me, and embarrassed because maybe he added his number just to see if I would text him, and now I have, he's probably laughing at me.

"I think we should go for Friday night drinks when we close up," suggests James. He's getting over another broken heart, at least the third one this month.

"I think you purposely screw up your relationships so you can force us all to drink with you," says Will.

"Like I have to force you." James scoffs, tussling his client's hair and giving Will a pointed look through the mirror reflection.

"I'm having a night in," I announce, flicking through the pages of a magazine. I've finished my bookings for the day and I'm waiting around to see if there are any walk-ins. The bell above the door tinkles, indicating a customer. I sigh and close the magazine.

"Another night in, you boring bitch," teases Henry. "I think you're trying to grow your virginity back."

"If that was possible, then trust me, it's fully back." I laugh, but it soon fades when I realise that Hawk is standing in the doorway by the front desk. "Oh . . ."

He smirks. "Hey, beautiful, thought I could do with a tidy-up. What do you think?" He runs his hands through his messy hair.

"Erm," I mumble, "sure, come this way."

He follows me over to an empty sink, I feel everyone's eyes on me as the six-foot-something, well-built biker takes a seat. I'm pretty sure this is a first in the salon's history. I place a cape around him with shaky hands, and I don't know why I'm so nervous. "Just lie back," I say, keeping my hand on his shoulder and gently guiding him back so his head rests on the edge of the sink.

"How've you been?" he asks casually.

"Oh, yah know, not bad. You?"

"Sorry I didn't get back to yah. I don't like technology. I can't work that shit."

"Oh, that's fine. I forgot, actually." I cough to cover up the fact that my face burns with embarrassment at my lie. I hold the shower head over his hair and run my fingers through it, allowing the warm water to soak it. He closes his eyes, giving me a chance to take in his chiselled profile. His beard is long but neat, and it covers some of the tattoos on his neck. The tatts trail under his shirt, and his arms are also covered. There's no space for new ones.

"They cover my chest too," he says, interrupting my ogling. I blush again and smile bashfully.

I begin to rub shampoo into his hair, massaging his scalp expertly, and he groans low and deep, closing his eyes again. I press my legs together tight, suppressing the throb that his groaning is causing between them. "You grew your virginity back?" He smirks, letting me know that he overheard my conversation.

I laugh. "Awkward."

"I like an experienced woman," he mutters. "Makes things much more fun."

I grab a clean towel. "All done," I announce a little too brightly, desperately trying to change the subject. He sits up, making the chair creak in protest. I begin to rub his hair with the towel. "Follow me."

I sit him in my cutting chair, and he smiles at me through the mirror. "You look flushed. You okay?" he asks.

"So, I'm just giving you a tidy-up?" I ask, and he nods.

"What time do you get off?"

"After she's finished with you," says Henry with a grin, and I scowl at him.

"Are you free for a drink?" asks Hawk.

"No," I begin, and Henry laughs aloud, cutting me off.

"Of course, she's free," he says.

"Thank you, Henry," I hiss, "as helpful as ever."

"What harm can it do?" asks Hawk. "Let's get a drink. No commitment, just a drink."

"I'm not sure it's a good idea," I say, snipping the ends from his hair.

"Because of Tanner?" he asks, and I meet his eyes in the mirror. "Because he says you're free, that you're not branded to him no more." My heart rate picks up at the thought of Tanner saying those words. "Last I heard, he was making a go of things with that pregnant bitch," he adds.

"Oh," I mutter, unsure of what else to say. "You spoke to Tanner?"

"I saw him a couple of days ago, hand-in-hand with the pregnant girl. Introduced her as his ol' lady."

I swallow the lump that had suddenly formed in my throat, my hands trembling. "Right," I mumble, trying hard to focus on Hawk's hair as it slides between my fingers.

"I thought you knew," he says, frowning. "I just figured, if he's telling me that shit, he's okay if I move in on you."

"Yeah, well, I sort of knew. Sort of. I had an idea. It's fine, I'm fine," I say, a little too forced. "Almost done." I add a fake smile.

I finish his hair with no memory of how I'd gotten through the cut, my mind completely full of images of Tanner and Melissa. I go off to wash my hands with Henry hot on my heels. "Oh my god, you did so well not to break down just then," he says sincerely. "Now, go for a drink with that gorgeous hot man and ride him until the early hours. Chances like this don't present themselves every day." He thrusts my jacket at me. "A man that size is going to have a huge cock. I'm so jealous right now. If you can get a photo, I'd be forever grateful."

"Aww, Henry," I groan, "you always ruin your nice words with smut."

He pushes me back out to where Hawk is waiting patiently. He looks more handsome with his hair trimmed and brushed back from his face. "You ready?" he asks.

"Of course, she is. Make sure you get her home safe, walk her inside, right into her apartment," Henry insists. "Tuck her in and all that."

"I intend to," says Hawk, holding his hand out. "Let's go." I hesitate before placing my hand into his and letting him lead me from the salon. We walk towards a wine bar at the end of the road, and I find myself constantly looking around, wondering if Tanner is watching even though I can't feel him around me. Maybe that's what happens when you spend time apart—you lose that in-tune vibe we once shared.

The bar is busy, and Hawk leads me to a table. "I'll go to the bar. Take a seat." I shrug out of my jacket, watching as he makes his way back through the crowd to the bar. People move out of his way, parting like a river for Jesus, and I smile to myself. He looks so out of place in this posh bar, and I wonder if he feels uncomfortable. Tanner would have. He hated these modern places.

Tanner

I watch the red dot flashing on my mobile. Heather's Wine Bar is just around the corner from Brook's workplace, so maybe she's gone for a drink with Henry and her work crew. Melissa approaches, and I shove my phone back in my pocket. She places a kiss on the side of my head and then lowers into the seat next to me. She's getting rounder every day, and simple tasks like sitting seem hard for her. "I'm so tired," she complains. "You really have to let me sleep tonight," she adds, winking.

I run my hand through her hair, gripping it at the base of her scalp and pulling her towards me so I can kiss her. "Not a chance, baby. I'm hard just thinking about tonight." She smiles against my mouth, opening slightly to give me access.

"Cooper was looking for you," she eventually says between kisses. I grope at her breast, and she grins. It amazes me that she wants rough sex even though she's heavily pregnant. "Unless you need to unwind before you see him?"

Smirking, I take her hand and pull her to her feet. "An offer I can't refuse."

As we pass Cooper's office, he pops his head out. "Tanner, I need a word," he says coldly.

"It'll have to wait, Pres. I have places to be," I say, equally as cold. I don't have to look at Melissa's face to know she's smirking. She seems to love the idea that she's coming between me and the club, especially me and my President. We're trying new tactics to see if she's really here because of the baby or if she has an ulterior motive.

CHAPTER TEN

Brook

"I was young and foolish. I thought dating a biker would make me cool." I laugh, and so does Hawk. "All it actually did was push my friends away. Tanner was intense and they didn't get him, didn't get us." I pause and then smile. "Sorry, it always comes back to Tanner. I don't mean to do it."

"It's fine. You were with him a long time, I get it," he says, sipping his whiskey.

"What about you? Any long relationships?"

"Not really. Messed-up childhood, scared of commitment, blah blah," he mutters. "Can I ask why you and Tanner split?" No matter what I change the subject to, Hawk always brings it back to me. He clearly isn't comfortable talking about himself.

"I had a messed-up childhood too. My parents weren't great. I spent a lot of time in and out of foster care." I'm sharing to prompt him, but I know by the look on his face that he isn't going to spill anything about his childhood. "We split because he cheated on me with the pregnant girl."

Hawk nods. "I suspected as much."

"Have you been cheated on?" I tried.

"Haven't we all?" he asks vaguely. "And now, you've covered up the tattoo."

I nod, the thought of my tattoo cover-up still raw. "It was another step in the right direction," I say. "How can I move on with his name on my body?"

"I'm surprised he let you," says Hawk.

"He didn't have a choice. I left the MC, I left Tanner, I'm free."

"Well, that makes me happy." He smiles. "If it wasn't so public here, I'd be kissing you round about now."

I glance around the many faces in the bar. "Why wait?" I flirt, the wine making me brave.

"I was hoping you'd say that." He grins, leaning towards me. His hand carefully cups my cheek and his lips brush against mine in a light, gentle kiss. He pauses, his eyes staring deep into my own, before taking the kiss deeper. It feels similar to Tanner, his beard brushing against my skin, his hands holding me close and making me feel safe, and the smell of whiskey and leather causing eruptions in my stomach.

When Hawk finally pulls back, I feel weak. It's been some time since I've had that warm butterfly feeling, and I smile at him shyly. "I know you're not the kind of girl to come back to the club with me after one kiss. I want you to know that I'm fucking hard for you right now, but I respect you enough to not push my luck." I watch his throat bob as he swallows the last of his drink. "So, I'm gonna walk you home and then get back to the club and have a cold shower." I feel disappointed but in an excited kind of way. "We'll be going on a second date," he confirms, standing and holding his hand out to me, "just so you know."

I head into work early on Saturday morning. Henry is already prepping for the day ahead. "There's a definite spring in your step," he observes, cocking a brow as I pass him.

"Don't be ridiculous, it was just a few drinks," I say coyly.

"Well, you won't be interested in a message I received last night." I pause and turn to him. "Mila," he adds, giving me a dramatic expression.

"Mila messaged you?" I asked, confused.

"She said to tell you she hasn't forgotten you. There is a very good reason for the silence and all will become clear but to trust her."

My first thought is that my phone is bugged. The Hammers are watching me, that's why Mila contacted Henry—she didn't want Cooper to see. "Did she tell you to tell me in person?" I ask, and he nods, confirming my suspicions. Thoughts of what Blake said spring to mind. What if they're watching to make sure I don't spill any club secrets, and if I did, would I be wiped out? And then anxiety gets the better of me and my thoughts turn wilder, like, if Cooper orders my kill, who would be the one to do it? Maybe Marshall? He was the least close to me. I shake my head, a shiver running down my spine. I'm being ridiculous. Cooper wouldn't have me killed, I'm almost certain. Besides, I don't know any club secrets, at least not ones big enough to bring them down.

Tanner

I sit at the large oak table. Cooper bangs the gavel on the table, declaring that church is now in session. "Okay, we have our suspicions about Melissa being here under false pretences," he begins. "We don't think she's here to hurt the club. It's personal to Tanner." All eyes fall to me, and I give a nod to confirm what Cooper is saying. "And so, we have a plan. Tanner has told Mel he wants to give things a go with her and the kid. One big happy family. Until we know what's going on, we keep her close to the club. I have guys watching her every move, but so far, nothing's really stood out apart from she likes to spend money, preferably Tanner's." A few laughs erupt. "We aren't ruling out that she has connections with Tanner's father. It's no secret that ties are frayed between the pair, and he's made it clear that he wants to make Tanner pay for past shit. I'll keep you updated, but keep your ears to the ground. You see or hear anything out of place, you come and see me."

After speaking with Kain and Cooper about my past and the abuse that I'd endured, we discussed the possibility that Melissa wasn't at our club by coincidence, that maybe she's here as part of my father's payback plot. My dad told Ma that he was playing out his payback right under our noses, and with my life going to shit lately, it all points to Mel and my breakup with Brook.

I've spent the last few days being the perfect gent, treating her to date nights, running her baths with rose petals and candles, shit that I never did for Brook . . . shit I should have done for her every day. I shake the thought away. I can't think about me and Brook right now, I have to get to the bottom of whatever Melissa's up to.

After church, I join Cooper and Mila with Mel at my side. We haven't told the girls about our suspicions, mainly because they can't keep secrets for shit. If we want to catch Melissa out, then it all needs to look real and having the other ol' ladies suddenly be nice to her would give the game away. Cooper's told Mila to cut ties with Brook for now because we're under threat from my dad and he doesn't want to drag Brook into it. The girls have accepted that for now and have so far agreed to no contact. They don't want to put her in danger by associating her with us.

"Mila, I ain't messing. You'll fucking accept Melissa just like the other ol' ladies," I growl. Mila glares back and forth between me and Cooper. I can see she wants to defy Cooper, but she's biting her lip, trying hard not to bring drama to him in front of us. Melissa smiles smugly, gripping my hand.

"And you'll advise the other ol' ladies to do the same," adds Cooper.

"You'd better get used to that couch," mutters Mila.

Cooper growls. "Fucking woman." She arches her brows higher.

"And kiss goodbye to baby number two cos that isn't happening." Then, she storms off.

"Thank you. It's nice to have people on my side for once," says Melissa, and she places a kiss on the back of my hand.

"They'll come around. Give her time to cool off," mutters Cooper before heading after his wife.

"Maybe he's finally accepting me too," Mel adds with hope in her voice.

"Maybe," I agree, wrapping an arm around her shoulders. "I have to go out for an hour. Go take a bath or something, and I'll join you when I get back."

"Going anywhere nice? I can come if you like," she offers.

"Not this time, baby. Go take that bath." I kiss her on the forehead and head out. She doesn't want to join me on this trip because it won't be ending well.

I tap on the door. Luckily, I followed another resident in because Brook never would have given me access if I'd buzzed her apartment. "Coming," she shouts from inside the apartment. I wait as she unbolts the door, leaning casually against the opposite wall. She sucks in a surprised breath when she sees me, and I smirk, glad I still take her breath away.

"You look good. Going out anywhere nice?" I ask, pushing off the wall and going inside her apartment without an invitation. She looks hot in a tight-fitting dress that reaches halfway down her tanned thighs. She slams the door and follows me.

"What are you doing here?" she demands, placing her hands on her hips.

I go in the kitchen, open her fridge, and pull out a cold beer. She doesn't usually buy beer in. "Who's the beer for?" I ask, popping off the cap and drinking it down. Her new rose tattoo has healed and is on show, peeking out from the low neckline of her dress. I reach out, and she stands rigid as I run a finger over the artwork.

"Have you come to kill me?" she blurts out, and I laugh.

"What?"

"You heard. Why are you here? How did you know I was here?"

"You live here. Are you on drugs, Brook?" I ask. Why the hell would she think I was here to kill her? "I came to sign the papers." As the words hit her, she flinches. "Just like you wanted," I remind her.

"What changed?" she asks, her voice almost a whisper.

"Where are you going looking all fancy?" I ask, ignoring her question. This is hard enough without me having to go into details.

"On a date," she says, eyeing me for a reaction.

I force the rage down, making my mouth form a smile and keeping my breathing even. "Great, well, now you'll have something to celebrate. Anyone I know?"

"Yeah, as a matter of fact, Hawk is taking me out again."

I pick up on two words, *Hawk* and *again*. I grip onto the worktop to avoid clenching my fists. "Again?" I repeat. "Second, third, or fourth date?" I ask.

She pauses and then shrugs. "Fourth," she says with a smile. It's a lie, I can see it in her face. She wants to get a reaction from me.

"It's his lucky night, fourth date rule and all that." I finish the beer, noticing the sadness on her face. She's falling for it, thinking I don't give a shit about her anymore. "So, papers?" I remind her.

"I'll just go fetch them." She wanders off into her bedroom.

The buzzer sounds. "I'll get that," I shout to her, picking up the intercom. It's tempting to tell Hawk to fuck off, but instead, I press the unlock button. Brook won't expect me to be nice, and it'll throw her.

I open the front door and head back into the kitchen. Hawk comes in a few moments later. "Tanner," he says, his eyes darting around the apartment, probably checking for Brook's body.

"She's just getting some paperwork," I say.

"Here it is," says Brook, coming to a stop when she spots us both standing awkwardly in her kitchen.

"Sorry, I didn't hear you buzz," she mutters, placing the papers onto the worktop.

Hawk steps towards Brook and places a kiss on her lips. The urge to rip his head from his body is overwhelming, so I focus on the envelope she's placed on the worktop, the one that's going to finalise everything between us. I fucking hate that envelope. "I'll just take this," I say, reaching for it.

"Oh, erm, can't you just sign it here? Then I can drop it off to my lawyer on Monday."

"I'd rather look over it, if you don't mind. It's not every day you get divorced."

"I haven't asked for anything, Tanner. It's straight forward." She's annoyed.

"Well, just to be sure, I want to go over it," I say coolly.

"I'm not like Melissa, I don't want anything from you," she hisses resentfully.

"Don't speak about my ol' lady like that, Brook. You know I don't stand for that shit," I growl, and her face pales. She blinks a few times and tears balance on her lower lashes. "I'll go look over these with Melissa, and then I'll sign and return them. Enjoy your date." I move closer, holding out my hand for Hawk to shake. "Good luck, man. She's a good one, so hold on to her."

He smiles. "Thanks, I intend to."

I stuff the envelope inside my kutte and head out the apartment, breathing a sigh of relief as soon as I step into the cold night air. Fuck, that was harder than I ever could have imagined and I swallow the lump in my throat. I haven't shed a fuckin tear since . . . I don't even remember but I'm damn close right now.

Melissa is laid out on our bed, her stomach stretched so tight that she looks fit to burst. I remember Kain telling me that seeing Harper pregnant with his kid made him hard, but I don't feel like that about Melissa. I watch as she runs her hand over her bump towards her breasts. "You took too long. I had to start without you," she grins, nodding towards the vibrator laying at her side on the bed.

"I went to get the divorce papers from Brook," I say, and her wandering hands still.

She pushes herself to sit. "Oh, right. What did she say?"

"Not a lot. She was surprised, especially because she was about to go on a date with a biker from another club."

"Right," she mutters, not looking at all surprised by that minor detail. "Anyone we know?"

"You wouldn't know him. Hawk, from The Devil Dogs."

"Well, forget about that for now. Let me distract you."

"She said she isn't taking anything from me. Ain't that weird?"

"Well, you don't have anything, do you?" she says, and it sounds more like a question than a statement.

"Nothing that she knows about."

"Oh yeah?" She sits up some more, swinging her legs over the edge of the bed.

"I have an account, but I haven't touched it, not ever. It's a payout I got from the state as a kid."

"Was it a lot of money?" she asks casually.

"I don't wanna talk about that now," I say, adding a smile. I stroke a hand over her hair and lean down to place a kiss against her mouth. She needs distracting, because her expression told me all I need to know—money is the real motive here.

"Tanner? Tan, are you in there?" Kain is banging on the bedroom door. I check the time and see it's two in the morning. Mel begins to stir next to me, so I get out of bed, pulling on my jeans, then step out of the room to find Kain pacing.

"Have you still got the app on your phone that follows Brook?" he asks, and I suddenly feel awake and alert.

"Yeah, of course. Hold on." I go back into the room to get my mobile before following Kain to Cooper's office downstairs. I open the app and relief floods me when the red dot flashes to tell me Brook is at home.

"She's at home, brother. What's happening?"

"She isn't home, Tanner. She went out on a date with Hawk. They left the bar hours ago, and Hawk managed to lose our tail. She hasn't been seen since."

"Well, maybe she went back to the Devils clubhouse?" I suggest, bitterness in my tone.

"No, we've been watching there. It's like they disappeared off the face of the earth, man. I'm worried."

"I'll call Hawk." I scroll through my phone until I find Hawk's mobile number and I press 'call'. It rings and rings, but he doesn't pick up. "I don't think we should worry too much. Brook is a big girl, and I'm pretty sure she's with him to pay me back. Who knows how far she'll go with that. Besides, if my dad's turned up, Hawk will protect her, man. I'm not worried."

I head back to bed with a niggling feeling in my gut. I lay down beside Mel, who snuggles next to me and mumbles something in her sleep. I shush her gently, praying she doesn't wake up because I can't face another round with her. She's insatiable, and quite honestly, it turns my stomach.

I toss and turn the rest of the night. As soon as the sun rises, I dress and head out on my motorbike. I need to see her for myself so I can relax, but when I get to her apartment, there's no answer on her intercom and Hawk doesn't pick up my call. I'm irritated but console myself with the fact it's only five in the morning and they're probably asleep somewhere . . . together. I decide to drive over to the Devils clubhouse. Surely, that's where they'd be.

There're remnants of a party coming to an end with a few guys lying about, surrounded by empty cans, and a firepit burning itself out. Low beats are playing from inside the club, and as I move closer, I notice Capone, the President, leaning against the wall having a cigarette. He recognises me too and pushes off the wall to shake hands. As he greets me warmly, I'm thankful for not having any bad blood between us.

"Hey, Tanner, what brings you here at this hour?"

"I'm looking for your VP," I say.

"You're out of luck, man. He called last night to say he was out of town for a few days. Didn't say much apart from his girl's dad was getting released soon and he needed to get some shit sorted."

"He didn't say where he was at?" Capone shakes his head and concern mars his face, but I don't want him getting involved, so I smile to put him at ease. "Not to worry. He's with my ex, and I wanted to bring the divorce papers to him as a sign of respect. Didn't want to approach her directly behind his back."

"You used to be with Mellie?" Capone asks, grinning. "I didn't know that. Must be a shitter to see her pregnant then. How long you been separated?"

"Mellie?" I repeat as my mind races.

"Yeah, Hawk's ol' lady, Melissa."

"I think we have crossed wires, man. My ex is Brook."

It's Capone's turn to look confused. "I don't know no Brook. Hawk's with Melissa and they have a kid on the way. You sure you got the right brother?"

I take a few steps back, his words causing my blood to run cold. "My mistake. Brook must be lying to me. Sorry, man." I go back to my motorbike and pull out my mobile. Cooper answers on the third ring,

"Shit, brother, have you seen the time?" he mumbles sleepily.

"Go to my room and keep Mel there until I get back. I've got news."

I hear Cooper stumble about, getting himself dressed. I wait patiently, listening while he opens and closes doors. Finally, he groans aloud. "She ain't in there, Tan."

"She has to be there. I left her half an hour ago and she was asleep. Check around. I'm heading back."

CHAPTER ELEVEN

Brook

Hawk pulls my hair as he unfastens the knot of the blindfold, and I flinch. It drops from my face, and I blink a few times while my eyes adjust to the light. "Hawk, what's going on?" I've been asking the same question, and each time, he's ignored me. I look around and find we're in some kind of cabin. It's small, and if I wasn't in this bizarre situation right now, I'd think it was romantic and cute. There's an empty log fire and a double bed. The curtains at the window are pulled together, but there's a slight gap where I can see trees, maybe a forest.

Hawk shrugs out of his leather jacket and sits on the double bed as I fidget on the hard wooden chair that I'm currently tied to. "What lengths would you go to for love, Brook?"

"Well, if you want my honest opinion, I think this is a little extreme, but I guess love sends people crazy." I use humour to cover the utter panic I'm feeling because not only did I not see where the hell I was going once we left town, but I know Tanner isn't watching me and he won't be able to find me, he won't even realise I'm gone. My eyes fall to my handbag, and I suddenly feel hope because I'm certain the Hammers were tracking my mobile, maybe Henry or James will alert them when they realise I'm not around. Hawk smirks when he sees where I'm looking.

Reaching for my bag, he opens it up and empties the contents onto the bed. "You really should be more careful where you leave your phone," he says, and I notice it doesn't spill out with the other things.

"It was in my bag," I mutter.

"Yeah, I might have slipped it out when I came to pick you up."

"What's going on?" I ask again.

"Unfortunately for you, you're collateral for something bigger."

Hawk's mobile buzzes and he smiles, answering the call. "Baby, where are you?" He falls silent while the other person replies. "Well, I thought you were leaving last night." His expression changes and he looks pissed. "Did you fuck him?" He stands and begins to pace. "You're a liar. I can tell by your voice, you've fucked him." He disconnects the call and throws his mobile onto the bed. "Fucking bitch," he growls to himself.

Hawk pulls out a small knife, and I hold my breath as he slices away the plastic ties holding my wrists. "Get on the bed," he orders menacingly. I hesitate, and he huffs. "Nothing like that. We need some sleep. It was a long drive." He pulls me by the arm and shoves me towards the double bed. I lie down stiffly, terrified of what he might do next.

I'm not even sure how the hell this all happened. One minute, we were having something to eat, and the next, he was inviting me back to his place. I agreed, mainly because I was mad at Tanner for being so fucking blasé about the divorce papers. I wanted to prove to myself I'm ready to move on, which is bullshit. I'm so not ready. I got on Hawk's motorbike, talking myself into the whole thing, but when I put my arms around him, he put cable ties around my wrists. He wouldn't answer my questions. He drove until my hands lost all feeling and then pulled over to put a blindfold over my eyes, all the while keeping silent. I'm so fucking confused.

I watch as Hawk kicks off his boots and then his jeans. He climbs into bed behind me and pulls the blanket over us. I stiffen, hardly believing he's acting so normal when, inside, I'm having a mental breakdown and working out how the fuck I'm gonna get out of this, whatever *this* is.

"I'm sorry for everything," he mutters, wrapping his heavy arm around my waist and pulling me against him. I shudder with repulsion. "Sometimes we get dragged into shit that we don't really want to be part of. I feel like we've both ended up here through making bad choices."

"I don't understand why I'm here," I whisper. "I didn't make a bad choice."

"It'll all become clear. Get some sleep. It's been a long night."

After a few minutes of laying in silence, I begin to drift off. The night's taking its toll on me, and even though I'm terrified, deep down, I'm praying to God that Tanner realises I'm gone and he comes looking for me.

"Well, well, well..." A female's voice brings me from a dream about Tanner. We were back together, and I was happy, but when I open my eyes and reality kicks in, I want to scream. I'm not back with Tanner. I'm in a cabin, in the middle of nowhere, and Melissa is staring down at me.

"Melissa?"

"Sleeping Beauty and my man, all cosy in my father's cabin."

I push myself to sit up, glancing around the cabin with hope that Tanner is here too. Hawk is still beside me with his arms behind his head and a smirk on his face.

"You finally arrived then," he says to Melissa.

"Pleased to see me, or is it waking up next to miss perfect that has you rock hard?" she demands to know. My eyes automatically go to the tent his erection is causing in his pants.

"How was Tanner when you left his bed?" he asks coldly.

"He was relaxed after a night of fucking," she hisses, and Hawk dives from the bed, standing toe to toe with Melissa.

"You're a bitch," he growls, and she smiles wide like she's receiving a compliment. She wraps her hands in his hair and stands on her tiptoes so she can place her lips on his. I watch in horror as they kiss frantically. "I missed you," he whispers against her mouth.

"I missed you too," she pants, then they pull apart. "We need to pick my father up at mid-day."

Hawk checks his watch. "We should make a move. What are we doing with her?" he asks, nodding in my direction.

"She's coming with. I don't wanna risk her getting away."

Tanner

"Keep your mobile phones on. If they've taken Brook, they'll contact us."

"What do they want with Brook?" asked Mila. She folds her arms across her chest and begins to pace the floor with worry marring her face. "I hope she's okay."

The club door flies open and Jase waltzes in, pulling my dad behind him. "Look who I found." He grins, shoving him towards us. Dad stumbles, clearly drunk, and I roll my eyes.

"Son, what's going on?" he asks, his eyes darting around nervously.

"Don't call me son," I spit. "Where's Brook?"

"Brook?" he repeats, sounding confused. "I don't know."

"You're behind this, I know you are, so spill before things get nasty," I warn.

"Carl, I don't know what you're talking about."

"You told Mum I was gonna pay. What did you mean?" He shakes his head again, and I lose my patience. "Get him out of my sight," I growl. Jase pulls him towards the door that leads to our basement. A few hours in the cold darkness might get him talking, and he'll need a drink by then.

I call Hawk for the hundredth time, but he doesn't answer, and I'm getting frustrated. It's been almost seventeen hours since Brook was last seen. I don't know if she's dead or alive, and I don't know why she's been taken. I try Melissa, and again, I get no answer. I snatch a bottle of whiskey from behind the bar. "Pres, give me ten, then follow me down," I say. He nods, and I head for the basement.

My dad is tied to a chair and he's shaking uncontrollably. He's been down here almost four hours, so he'll be craving alcohol. His tired, bloodshot eyes reach mine and then they fall to the bottle that I wave at him, a cruel smile on my face. "I don't need to get the heavy tools out for you, daddy dearest, I just need to show you this," I say.

He groans. "What do you want from me?"

"I know you're behind all of this. Where's Brook?"

"I don't know," he hisses through clenched teeth. I unscrew the cap slowly and his eyes are drawn back to the bottle.

"I'll give you a minute to think." I smile cruelly and take a long pull of the amber liquid. I close my eyes in pleasure. "Tastes so good."

"I don't know where she is," he yells, pulling at his restraints. "Carl, stop this bullshit."

"What I don't get is why now? You've had years, so why now?"

"I don't know what you're talking about. Does your mum know about this?"

"Ma doesn't care. She's living her best life now that you've gone. I've done up the house, replaced the furniture, and I've never seen her look so happy." I take another swig, moving closer so he can smell the alcohol.

"She'll take me back in a heartbeat," he hisses, and I laugh. I've had the conversation with her, and she's done with him. She loves being around me and the club. The ol' ladies have welcomed her as one of our own, so she's never short of company, and whenever she gets lonely at home, she comes to the club. "Maybe Brook left your ass for something better," he adds.

"Yeah, maybe. Once she tells me that herself, I'll let you go. Until then, you're stuck in here with me, old man."

"Does she know about your lies?" His smug face pisses me off and I hold the bottle over his head, pouring some of the whiskey over him. He closes his eyes, the smell gripping his senses and making sure his mind is on his next drink.

"They weren't lies and you know it. I've had years to think it over, and yah know what I came up with? I think you felt bad. He was your mate, and it turns out, he wasn't as great as you thought. He was a dirty bastard, and you hated being wrong. By the time everything came out, you were too deep in with him, you couldn't risk people thinking you were like him, so it was easier to make everyone believe that I was a troubled kid, a liar."

Dad smirks, and I get a glimpse of the cold darkness behind his eyes. "He said you loved it, that you were fucking gay and he was teaching you a lesson. You were the pervert!"

I laugh, hardly daring to believe my ears. "I was a kid. Don't you think that if I was gay, I'd be with a man and not my wife?"

"I think Kenny healed you. He made you a better man, and you should be thanking him."

I take another drink and shake my head in disappointment. The man is delusional. I learned a long time ago that the abuse I suffered was not my fault and my father's reaction to the whole situation was his problem, not mine. "Yah know, I might just leave you to fester down here."

The door opens and Cooper steps in. He holds a bottle of vodka, my dad's tipple of choice. "I've just heard some interesting news, brother," he says, moving closer while unscrewing the vodka cap.

"Yeah?" I ask.

"Seems Kenny Montgomery was released from jail an hour ago." My smile fades. It wasn't what I was expecting and yet I could kick myself. It makes sense, that's why all of this is happening now. Kenny is the ringleader.

"And so, the pieces fall into place," says Dad, grinning wide.

I can't hold back anymore. My fist smashes into his face and I savour the sound of his nose crushing as it breaks. Blood pours from it as he laughs, letting it coat his teeth. "Never could quite control that temper, but I guess it's how I bred you, to fight. If you'd have controlled that temper, you could have made it professional."

"You made me fight grown men," I growl angrily. "Don't pretend you were some kind of coach, showing his son how to fight. You took bets on kids beating the shit out of each other, and when that didn't make enough money, you put me in the ring with men. You're sick!"

"You were hungry for the fights, boy. Don't make out you didn't enjoy being in there with those men. You're the sick one."

Cooper puts the vodka to Dad's lips and allows him a sip. "You can have this whole thing, and we'll let you go on your merry little drunken way, if you tell us what the hell is going on."

"I can't believe you haven't worked it out yet." He laughs, mocking us. "Melissa isn't yours, Carl. She belongs to Hawk. The baby, it's his. You stupid fuck, believing you slept with someone else. You were so easy to fool."

I exchange a look with Cooper. That confirms that Hawk is a part of this too, and what Capone said was true—the kid isn't mine. "So, what's the connection with those two and Kenny?"

"When you spouted your lies, you cost a little girl her father. He was her hero, and you took him away with your evil bullshit."

"Melissa?" I mutter. "Melissa is Kenny's daughter?" Sickness burns my throat.

"Shit," mutters Cooper. "We did all the checks and that didn't come up."

"You think Hawk is stupid? He knew you'd check her out, so he wiped her files and recreated them. You think you're all invincible, that you're the only guys who can make people disappear."

"So, what do they want with Brook?" I ask.

"To know that, you'll have to wait for Kenny's call. He'll tell you what he wants in return for that stupid little bitch. She was so desperate to get over you, she fell for Hawk without him even trying. Boy, did he laugh about her."

I punch him again, needing him to shut the fuck up. "Where are they?" asks Cooper, and Dad shrugs. I snatch the bottle of vodka from Cooper and begin to empty it on the floor. My father cries out like he's in physical pain. "A cabin! It's a cabin," he blurts out.

"I don't know where, I swear I don't." I throw the bottle against the far wall and smile with satisfaction as it shatters into pieces.

"I want him dead by this evening," I mutter, and then I leave.

Cooper runs to catch up with me. "I'll get Specs on it. He should be able to find this cabin. You get the guys together and fill them in. We need everyone in for this."

Needing air, I head outside. I light up a cigarette and lean back against the wall, inhaling deeply. The relief that Melissa isn't pregnant with my kid is overwhelming. I didn't cheat on Brook. All this heartache and I didn't do anything wrong. Bitterness builds up. She didn't deserve any of this pain. Neither of us did.

My phone rings and I pull it from my pocket. The number is withheld. I press it to my ear but remain silent, trying to pick out any background noises.

"Want to play a game, Carl?" Kenny Montgomery's voice still has the power to make me freeze with fear. Those words . . . those six words bring bile to my throat as buried memories rush to the forefront of my mind. I clench my fists and squeeze my eyes shut. I take a deep breath and release it slowly. When I open my eyes again, I'm ready for the fight. I've waited years for this.

"I'm a little old for you these days, Uncle Kenny," I say calmly, using the name he forced me to use when I was a kid. "I could probably show you a trick or two, to be honest."

"I have someone here who wants to speak with you."

There's a muffled cry followed by Brook's voice. "Get the fuck off me, you piece of crap," she screams, and I smile at the venom in her voice. That's my girl, not showing fear.

"It's been a while since I felt a good pair of tits, Carl," he whispers, his tone mocking, and Brook lets off a few curse words.

"Really? I thought cock was more your thing. Bet you got plenty of that inside. Yah know, I felt your daughter's last night, although I hate fake tits. They're just not quite the same as the real thing." I keep my tone flat, like I'm bored.

Kenny chuckles, and it causes the hairs on the back of my neck to stand up. "You loved our time together. You were crying out for attention and that's what I gave you. It hurt me when you turned against me and made up those lies."

"Cut the bullshit, Kenny. What do you want?"

"I want you to feel the pain I felt when they locked me up. I had to listen to my baby girl crying for me, knowing I couldn't be there to watch her grow up."

"Please," I mutter. "I saved her. Who knows what the fuck you'd have done to her if you'd been left to it? And don't you think I fucking suffered, having your hands on my body? If you were so concerned about Melissa, you'd have kept your head down and done the five years. Instead, you were a dick and got time added. That ain't on me. Brook has nothing to do with this. We're divorcing, thanks to you and your crazy daughter. You got what you wanted."

"Oh, don't worry, I'm not after your pretty little wifey, It's the money I want. The state paid you a good amount, and without me, you wouldn't have gotten that."

"Fuck, you want me to thank you for abusing me?" I ask dryly. The payout came after an investigation was carried out into the police who dealt with the case. Kenny would have spent longer in jail for what he'd done to me if evidence hadn't gone missing. I put that cash in the bank and it's been there since. I never touched a penny of it.

"You can have the damn money. It means nothing to me. But you let Brook go without a hair on her head out of place."

"I call the shots around here. Get me the money and call me when it's done. And Carl, don't involve the police or your precious club. If I get wind you've fucked this up, I'll be visiting your President's nephew. Asher's a little cutie."

"What the fuck is wrong with you?" I yell.

"How important is he to you, Carl?" he asks, laughing.

"Precious enough to rip your head clean off your body for even mentioning his name," I growl.

"Then make it quick. I want that money." The line goes dead.

"Fuck," I yell. "Fuck, fuck, fuck!"

CHAPTER TWELVE

Brook

I feel dirty, like I need to wash this place from me. They dragged me out to pick up Melissa's dad from prison. I was blindfolded and shoved into the boot of the car. And since we've been back, Melissa and her dad have been outside the cabin catching up, leaving me and Hawk alone. "I thought you were a nice guy," I say, my voice dripping with disappointment.

"I am," he says defensively. "I told you, we both got caught up in shit we had no control over. If I could get you out of this, I would."

"I can't believe I was considering you as a potential boyfriend."

"You were?" he asks, sounding surprised.

"And don't pretend you couldn't get me out of this if you really needed to. You could kill these motherfuckers in a second."

"I could," he admits, "but she's pregnant with my kid."

"You sure it's yours? Cos she told Tanner it was his too, and we all believed that. She's a good liar. How do you know she's not fooling you?"

He ponders over my words for a moment before shrugging. "Let's talk about you."

Right now, he's the last person I want to talk to. "I'm not telling you anything else, Hawk."

"Why were your parents so rubbish? Did they want you? Were you planned?"

I form a part-lie, hoping to divide his loyalties. "I wasn't planned. My mum tricked my dad, saying she couldn't get pregnant. When she did, he was angry. It caused lots of problems between them."

Hawk's eyes dart to the open door, where Melissa is sitting on the swing chair with her dad. "Did they mistreat you?"

"They neglected me, too wrapped up in their problems and turning to drink and drugs." I lower my voice. "Melissa was quite the party animal before she got pregnant, wasn't she? She was always drinking at the club."

Hawk ignores me. "My parents didn't want me either. I went into foster care as a baby and never knew what it was like to have a real family."

I change tactics. "It's cute you want that for your kid. You'll make a great dad."

"You think?" he asks, looking hopeful, and I nod.

"I'm not sure about Melissa, though. I mean, kidnapping another woman to help exact revenge," I shrug, "not really mother material."

"She loves her dad." Hawk sighs, rubbing at his face with an exhausted look in his eyes.

"More than she loves you and this baby?" I ask, raising my eyebrows. "I know I'd never let anyone come between me and a baby. I've wanted it for so long."

Melissa comes back into the cabin and glances between us suspiciously, "Everything okay?"

"Yeah. How's my boy today?" asks Hawk, placing his hand on her bump. She moves out of his reach, looking uncomfortable.

"What are you two talking about?"

"Kids," I say, smiling. "How some parents were cut out for the job and others not so much."

"Oh yeah, like who?" she asks, folding her arms and glaring at me.

"You, your dad," I say coldly. "Fucking young children doesn't make the ideal grandpa," I add. Melissa slaps me hard across the face, and I wince before forcing a smile. "I heard the conversation between your dad and Tanner. He likes little boys. Aren't you having a boy?"

"Tanner is gay," she shouts. "He tried it on with my dad, and when he rejected him, Tanner lied."

"Gay?" I repeat. "I think we both know that isn't true."

Kenny rushes in, grabbing my upper arm and hauling me to my feet. He pushes his face into mine. "If you don't shut your mouth, I'm going to show you exactly what I did to your precious Tanner," he growls.

I smirk. "I'm not scared of you," I lie, feeling absolutely terrified inside.

He punches me hard in the stomach, and I fold over, coughing.

"Well, you should be, little lady. You should be, because I have nothing to lose and you have everything." I don't miss the hurt on Melissa's face as he shoves me back onto the bed.

I wake suddenly and the cabin is in darkness. I'm lying on the hard floor while Hawk and Melissa are in the double bed and Kenny is on the couch. The thin sheet they gave me is doing nothing to keep me warm, and I pull myself to sit, hugging my knees to my chest.

"Are you okay, baby?" whispers Hawk. He's acting like none of this is happening, like this is normal. I ignore him because the last thing I need is Melissa or her father waking up. "Brook?"

"What?" I whisper coldly.

"Are you okay?" he repeats.

"No, I'm here against my will, I'm cold, and I have a cramp from laying on this hard floor," I hiss. I watch as he carefully rises from the bed and reaches down a hand to me. I take it, and he helps me to stand. I'm so stiff, I almost groan aloud.

"Follow me," he whispers, keeping hold of my hand and leading me outside. In his other hand, he's holding a large grey sweater. He helps me to put it on, and I snuggle into it gratefully. It's huge on me and comes to my knees, but at least it'll help to keep me warm. The scent of his aftershave lingers on the material and it reminds me of happier times when I first met him.

"Hawk, what's gonna happen to me?" I whisper. He lowers onto the swing chair and tugs me down beside him. I pull my knees to my chest and tuck my legs into the sweater.

"I don't know. It's all gotten out of hand," he admits, pulling out a cigarette and lighting it.

"You could change this. You could help me." I rest my head on his shoulder, hoping he'll feel sorry for me.

He gives me a side glance and then shakes his head and gives a low laugh, "Yeah, and have your old man come after me?"

"He isn't my old man. We split up. That's why I was going on dates with you, remember," I say bitterly. "I was just trying to move on from Tanner and you screwed me over."

"I know you probably won't believe me, but you grew on me, Brook. If things were different . . ."

I sit straighter, taking hold of his arm. "But things can be different. You can make all of this go away, and we can go back how it was. We were getting on so well, I really felt like we were going places."

He stares straight ahead, sucking on his cigarette until the tip burns bright, "It's too late. We've come too far."

"What do you get out of any of this? Because even if they kill me, Tanner will still come for you all."

"Hopefully, I'll be far away. Once Kenny pays us, we're out of here."

"You're leaving your club? For a woman?" I laugh. A real biker wouldn't ever be swayed by a woman—the club comes first. "Wow."

"Mel doesn't want our kid growing up in the club. I don't blame her."

"I don't believe you," I say indignantly. "It's in your blood. You're doing this because you think it will make her happy, but what about you? Where will you go when the crying baby is too much? There'll be no jumping on your motorbike and riding off into the sunset for a few weeks."

"That's okay. She's all I need."

"Bullshit," I mutter. "I know you liked me, Hawk. I felt it too. If you and she were that serious, your head wouldn't have turned."

He shrugs. "I hadn't seen her in weeks, and it was tough. You just happened to be there."

I place my hand on his knee, and he stares down at it. "I don't believe that, Hawk. When you kissed me, everything else melted away." I run my tongue over my lip as his eyes follow the movement. I move closer to him, and his expression becomes heated. Resting my hand on his cheek, I run my thumb over the bristles of his beard before gently placing my lips on his, "I know you felt it," I whisper against them, gently biting his lower lip, "but now, you'll never know what it was like."

"What?" he mutters.

"Fucking me," I whisper, and he sucks in a breath. "Promise me, if they decide to kill me, you'll give me one time." I press my lips against his again, and this time, it's harder and more forceful. His hands run up my arms and then cup my face.

"Brook, what the fuck are you doing to me?" he groans against my mouth. I run my hand farther up his thigh and stop next to his groin. "Brook," he whispers, and I'm not sure if his tone is desperate or warning, but I continue to move my hand until it's rubbing against his erection. He throws his head back and closes his eyes. "Shit, you're gonna turn me into a damn teenager if you keep doing that."

"We could have this all the time, Hawk, just me and you," I remind him. I climb over him, straddling his lap. He grips my thighs, and I hold onto his shoulders. "If we were alone right now," I whisper, keeping my lips close to his ear, "I'd be sucking your cock." He hisses again, and I begin to rub myself against him, keeping my breasts close to his chest as I move myself back and forth.

I guide his hands up my body, making sure they brush over the curve of my breasts. "We have to stop this. I want to fuck you so bad," he whispers desperately.

I pull the sweater up over my stomach, exposing my lace-encased breasts, and he groans louder. "We could slip away, make the most of our last few hours together. They'll never know."

Hawk grips my thighs hard, and I still. "I know what you're doing."

I smile innocently. "I just need to fuck you, Hawk, or we'll never know what we could have had. We'll always be wondering."

"You want to find a way to escape, and if I take you away from here, you'll run."

"I won't," I say sincerely. "You can tie me up if it makes you happier, but I'd never be able to outrun you. I'm not stupid."

"I can't take you anywhere."

"Not even for this?" I ask, grabbing his hand and moving it to my pussy. He presses over my jeans, and I whimper, like I'll die if he doesn't fuck me now.

"Baby, don't do this to me," he groans. "I can't take you anywhere. If Kenny wakes, he'll kill us both."

I sigh and climb from his lap. "Fine, if you're scared of Kenny, then forget it." I pout for added effect and then move to the steps and sit down. It's one step more away from him and closer to freedom. I stare out to the trees that surround us. I have no clue which way to run, but I think heading for the thickest part would be best because I'm small, so I can slip through the trees and hide easily. Hawk is too big and will fall and stumble.

"I'm not scared of Kenny," he growls.

"Sounds like it," I mutter. "Better check he isn't listening to all this. He might kill you," I mock as I glance back. Hawk is lighting another cigarette, and I see my chance. I leap from the wooden steps and take off without looking back, running for the thickest part of the trees, guided by the shimmering moonlight.

"You stupid bitch," I hear him growl, and his heavy footfalls tell me he's right behind me. I realise all too late that it's tricky to run through a wooded area at night, and it's so much darker than I imagined. I jump over a fallen tree and break out into a clearing. It's lit by the moon, and as my foot hits the soft grass, I slip on its dampness and crash to the floor. Hawk is on me before I even realise I'm down. I cry out in frustration, hitting my fists against the ground. His mouth is close to my ear. "Calm yourself. At least we're alone now."

I wriggle and push up from the ground, trying desperately to buck him off me, but it's no use, he's too heavy. "I told Melissa it was stupid to leave you alone with the little bitch. I knew she'd play you." Kenny's voice causes us both to freeze. "Did she blind you with her beauty?" he asks mockingly. Hawk pushes off me and stands. "Well, don't let me stop you, big man. What was gonna happen next?" I also stand, and Kenny grabs my arm, digging his fingers into the flesh. "Well, weren't you about to fuck?"

"No," says Hawk, "I was just gonna bring her back."

"Don't lie. You've got that look in your eye, the one all men get when they're about to turn feral." Kenny moves his hand to my hair and grips it tight. With his free hand, he pulls at the button on my jeans. "So, let's carry on."

I push his hand away, and he tugs my head back harder. "Please," I beg, trying to prize my hair from his grip.

"Please what?" he demands. "Hawk, get over here and finish what you started," orders Kenny.

"Nah, man, that isn't what we agreed."

"If you don't, then I will." He manages to unfasten the button and begins to push down my jeans as I fight with everything I have.

"Please, Hawk. Please don't let him hurt me," I beg.

"Look, Kenny, come on. What if Mel hears us?" Hawk tries.

"Don't pretend we're good men now, Hawk. It's been a long time since I've had a tight little pussy. Now, hold her still." Kenny shoves me towards Hawk, who luckily catches me, guilt plaguing his expression. I plead with my eyes for him to help me. "Let's get this over with, shall we," says Kenny, unfastening his belt. "Lay her down."

"Hawk, please, don't do this. We had something. You know we did." He looks pained, glancing between me and Kenny.

"Care to explain that little statement?" Melissa steps into the clearing. "What the fuck is going on?"

"Things are getting out of control, Mel," says Hawk.

"You'd better let her go and come back to the cabin with me. My dad can deal with her." She turns back towards the direction of the cabin, and Hawk mouths the word 'sorry' before releasing me to go after Melissa.

"No," I cry, "Hawk, please." He disappears into the trees.

Kenny sneers. "Wanna play a game, Brook?"

Tanner

I watch Mum to try and gauge her reaction. She clasps her coffee cup with a lost look on her face. "I just thought you should know," I tell her.

"Was it quick?" she asks, and I nod. I don't tell her that he suffered, that Kain took his time killing Dad slowly. She takes a deep breath and then plasters a smile on her pale face. "Well, that's that then."

"It's okay to be upset, Ma." I sigh. "You've been together a long time."

"He didn't treat me good, though, did he, Carl, so I shouldn't be sad. After everything he did, after the way he treated you, he doesn't deserve my tears."

"No, I don't think he does," I admit, "but I wasn't married to him. Marriage is complicated, and I don't have the right to tell you how you should feel. Cooper said I shouldn't tell you, that we should just say he ran away again, but I wanted you to know that he won't ever be coming back. I didn't want you to wait for him." Cooper wasn't happy about me coming here. He's worried Mum might tell the Police if they ever come looking, but she's been through enough and she deserves the truth.

"I won't tell anyone, Carl. You come first, and I'll protect you no matter what. I failed you all those years ago and I won't do that again, so if anyone asks, I shall tell them that he's run away like he always does."

I lean over, kissing her on the cheek, "I love you, Ma."

"I love you too. Any news on Brook?"

I shake my head. I can't tell her about Kenny, or what's happened with Brook and Melissa. It'll break her heart. I've made an appointment with the bank to withdraw the money, and I've left Kenny a message to ask him where and when he wants to meet. "I have to go. I have an appointment. If you need me, just call."

She walks me to the door. "I'm so proud of you, Carl," she says, squeezing my hand and smiling. I return the smile and then head out to my motorbike. It's not every day you tell your mum you've had your dad killed and she responds by saying she's proud.

The bank manager checks and rechecks my identification and the amount on the withdrawal slip. "That's a large amount to be withdrawing in one transaction, Mr. Tanner. Are you closing the account with us?"

"Yes," I say bluntly. I want my money and I'm not interested in small talk. He nods before disappearing to sort it out. I sit back in the grey padded chair and glance out the office window into the fancy bank. It's busy and full of people in suits. It's so out of my comfort zone that I often think that's the main reason I never touched this money. I have no doubt the interest on the account has increased the figure massively in the years it's been sat there.

The bank manager returns carrying my duffle bag, which is now full of bank notes. Once everything is signed, I head back out to my motorbike and check my mobile phone. Kenny's texted an address just an hour out of town. I forward the address to Kain, telling him that if he hasn't heard from me in an hour, he should come there to find me. I haven't told the MC about the latest development. Not with Kenny threatening Asher.

By the time I pull off the main road and onto a dirt track, it's getting dark. Up ahead, there's a small log cabin. There're no signs of life, but I stop just up the way and get off my motorbike. Making sure my gun is in place, as well as the two knives I have,

I slip the duffle bag onto my shoulder and make my way through the trees on foot. As I get closer, I see the embers of a cigarette. I can just make Kenny out, sitting on the steps of the cabin.

"You made it," he says as I get closer.

I hang back. Seeing him again makes my blood run cold. He looks no different than he did all those years ago, just thinner with less hair. "Where is she?"

"You got so big." He smirks, flicking his cigarette onto the ground. "I should warn you that there is a gun trained on you. Any sudden movements and you're a goner."

"Cut the crap, Kenny. Where's Brook?"

"She's a feisty one, that girl. Full of fire. Although when I left her an hour ago, she was a little less fiery and a whole lot more damp."

"What the fuck's that s'posed to mean?"

"Got the cash?"

I throw the bag to the ground in front of me, "You have to come and get it."

"I can't believe you actually came with the cash and without your backup. Are you stupid?"

"I don't have time for this bullshit, Kenny. Where's Brook?"

"She's safe. I'm gonna count that cash and then make the call."

"Until I see her, you aren't touching the cash. You have a short amount of time left before the Hammers are all over this place, so make that call and get her here now."

"Hawk, come count this money," shouts Kenny, and from the shadows, Hawk appears, his gun trained on me. I smile.

"Don't do anything stupid, Tanner," he warns.

"Oh man, you know I'm gonna kill you, right? There is no way you're walking away from here today."

"I've got the gun, dickhead," he snaps. He bends to collect the bag, and I grin wider as I bring my boot up and smash it into his face. I hear his nose crack, and then he falls backwards and the gun flies from his hand. "I'm assuming this was your guy with the gun, seeing as I'm still breathing," I say to Kenny.

He doesn't look fazed, and I realise this was probably all part of his plan. I don't let that deter me as I lay into Hawk, repeatedly punching him in the face until he's a bloody and unrecognisable mess. "You really do have anger problems, Carl," says Kenny with amusement.

"I wonder why," I mutter, pulling a knife from my boot and dragging it across Hawk's throat. He gurgles and blood spills from his mouth as he tries desperately to suck in another breath. I wipe my sweaty brow on the back of my bloodied hand and step back, dropping his lifeless body to the floor. Piece of shit.

"Where's Brook?" I ask again, and this time when I look up, it's Kenny with a gun pointed at my head.

"Throw me the bag."

A loud bang rings out and birds fly from the trees in panic. Kenny lurches forward and tumbles down the steps, landing in a heap on the ground. "Shit," I growl, racing over to him. Kain steps forward. "What the fuck, Kain," I yell, turning Kenny onto his back. He's gasping for breath, but he manages to smile up at me. "Where is she?" I demand.

"You'll never know," he whispers.

"Fuckkkkk!" I yell out, punching him hard. "Kain, what the hell were you thinking? Now, we'll never find Brook."

"Sorry, brother, I just saw the gun pointed at you and lost it. Why didn't you tell us you were meeting Kenny?"

"Because he made threats to Asher. Jesus, Kain, I told you not to come yet. I had this!"

I begin to pace back and forth. "Sorry, man. You'd better call this in. Cooper will lose his shit when he knows you've kept this from him."

Kenny coughs, and I reach for him. Pulling my knife back out, I push it slowly into his groin, and his eyes widen in shock. I smile as I twist it. I've waited years to do that. A sick satisfaction washes over me as he goes limp in my arms, his last breath laboured and painful.

I search both bodies but find nothing. Kain kicks the door in to the cabin, but it's empty. Kain calls Cooper and fills him in, and I hear his yelling from where I stand a few metres away. When Kain finally hangs up, he shrugs. "He said to check their mobile history. Maybe the maps app could lead us to where they've been the last few days."

I pull out Kenny's phone and use his thumb to open the lock screen. Sure enough, there's an address saved into his map app, which is another cabin a couple of hours from here.

CHAPTER THIRTEEN

Brook

Kenny and Hawk left us hours ago. It was light then and now it's dark. I pull a blanket from the couch and wrap myself in it. For the last twenty minutes, Melissa has complained nonstop about stomach cramps. I have no energy to even respond to her, and quite honestly, I don't care. She puffs again, and I roll my eyes.

"I think I'm in labour," she snaps.

"I'm not a nurse," I say dryly.

"I don't understand what's taking them so long. It was simple—get the cash and come back for me."

"If they were meeting Tanner, they'll be dead. Or maybe they've changed their minds about cutting you in and they've left. Hawk was having doubts."

Melissa eyes me suspiciously. "You're just trying to cause trouble. Ouch," she shouts out and bends slightly. "I really think I'm in labour."

"Well, you'd better pray they hurry back because I'm not helping you."

"You're such a bitch," she huffs. "You never liked me. From the second I stepped into the club, you looked down your nose at me."

I don't think that's true. I always welcome everyone to the club. "I didn't even notice you until you were all over my husband."

"He wasn't exactly pushing me away," she retorts, and I laugh.

"It was a lie, Melissa. He didn't touch you!"

"I know. How weak was your relationship, though, that you just took my word for it? Both of you did. It's sad really."

"It's pathetic the lengths you went to for a bit of cash. Your dad pimped you out to a man he abused as a child. Fucked up."

"He did not abuse him. Tanner lied," she yells.

"What makes you think Kenny is such a great guy?" I ask. "You hardly know him. You saw back in the woods, he was going to rape me."

"But he didn't."

"Only because Tanner messaged him about the money." I've never been so relieved in all my life.

Tanner couldn't have timed the text message any better.

Melissa shouts out, gripping her stomach. "The pain is coming every few minutes. Doesn't that mean the baby is coming soon?"

"I have no idea. Do not have it here in this cabin, cos I'm really not helping you."

"Hawk will be back any minute," she mutters, glancing out the window.

"You're so stupid. They've left you. They aren't coming back."

"Shut up," she yells and then cries out in pain again.

I turn my back to her. The last thing I want to do is help her, but if this baby decides it's coming, I can't just leave her to it. I groan. "Lay on the bed," I say through gritted teeth. I rip back the sheets so she can lie down, and she edges back onto the bed and slowly lays down. "Just so you know, I really don't want to help you."

"You don't really have a choice." Kenny left a gun in Melissa's care, telling her to aim and shoot if I decide to run. He also locked us inside the cabin, so the thought of him not returning isn't ideal. While Melissa removes her underwear, I think of ideas on how to escape once this baby has arrived, like shooting out the lock maybe.

"Okay, I'm ready," she announces.

"For what? I'm not looking down there," I say. "Just have a feel, see if it's different."

Before she gets a chance to reply, another pain rips through her and she screams. "They're getting worse," she cries. "I can't do this without drugs."

"Well, thanks to your dad and boyfriend, we're locked in here, so unless you have a secret stash of gas and air, you're doing this au naturel. He left you a gun, so I guess you can always shoot yourself if it gets too much," I suggest.

"Wow, you really are a bitch," she hisses, puffing through another pain.

"Only to women who make up lies to ruin my relationship and then kidnap me and hold me against my will. Usually, I'm really nice."

I sit back, watching her puff and pant. "I don't think the baby should come this quick. They told me I'd probably be in labour for hours with the first."

"How long have you had pains? Did you get a backache?"

"Well, yeah . . . I didn't know it was labour, though. I've been having backaches for days." She pants again, throwing her head back and groaning.

"What are you going to do if they've left you with no money and a kid?"

"This baby was an accident. I'll leave it on the hospital steps."

My heart aches. I've wanted a baby for so long, and here she is, just dumping her baby because it was unplanned. "Selfish cow," I mutter.

"How am I going to take care of a kid? Especially if you're right and they don't come back." She screams and then follows it up with a string of curse words. "Fuckkk, I've got a really weird feeling."

I go over to the bed and peer cautiously between her open legs. "Erm, I think I see something," I say, screwing up my face. Amongst all the blood, there's something which I assume is the top of the head.

Melissa looks panicked. "Oh Christ, I'm going to have a baby in a bloody cabin, in the middle of nowhere, with a woman who hates me."

I hear a low rumble from outside and shush Melissa, who scowls at me. "I hear something." I rush to the window and, sure enough, there're two motorbikes coming up the path. It's hard to tell from this distance whether they belong to Hammers men or Devils, but I pray it's someone who wants to help me get out of here.

"I told you Hawk would be back," pants Melissa, but I don't reply. I watch the bikes come to a stop and smile, the sight of Kain and Tanner pulling off their helmets bringing relief and then tears.

Tanner sees me and marches over, pressing his hands against the glass. "Baby." His intense stare warms my heart, and I place my hands to the glass to match his. I've never felt such relief.

"Am I glad to see you," I say, letting the tears run down my cheeks. "The door's locked."

"Not a problem," he announces. Seconds later, he kicks the door and it springs open. His chest heaves and his hands hang by his sides. His eyes are fixed on me, burning with mixed emotions, and his nostrils flare. "Here," he growls, and I run towards him, throwing myself into his arms. He sweeps me up with no effort, and my feet dangle as he buries his nose into my hair. "Fuck, I missed you," he whispers.

"I didn't think you'd ever find me out here."

"I'll always find you," he says, kissing my temple. "Always."

"I hate to break up the reunion but . . ." Kain trails off, and I follow his gaze to Melissa, who is deep breathing her way through another contraction.

"She's having a baby." I shrug. Tanner lowers me to the ground and takes me by the hand.

"Fuck her. Leave her here to have her damn baby. She isn't our problem."

"Man, you can't leave a woman in labour out here. What's wrong with you?" snaps Kain, heading towards Melissa and then screwing his face up and taking a few steps back. "Damn, that don't look good."

"Don't be looking there," yells Melissa, trying to cover herself up.

"Okay, let's all take a breath. We can't move her now and we can't leave her. Are Kenny and Hawk likely to come back?" I ask, and Kain shakes his head. "Right, so we're gonna have to help her."

"Are you shitting me, after what's she's done? She lied, ruined us," snaps Tanner.

I place a hand on his cheek. "But she didn't win in the end. She's gonna be stuck with a baby she doesn't want, no dad, no man, no money. She'll get her karma."

"Did those bastards take the money and run?" she pants, balling her fists as the pain builds again.

"Forget them. Let's get this baby out, so we can get you to hospital." I take a look and see the baby's head crowning. "I'm no expert, but I reckon you need to get pushing on the next contraction. Do you guys want to wait outside?"

They both step outside, and I go to the sink and wash my hands. I've never done this before, and I'm shaking with nerves. As I dry my hands, Melissa begins to growl and push.

Tanner

I hear the screams from inside and the reality hits me that I may not ever hear Brook go through that. It hurts my heart. I light another cigarette and take a long pull. "What do we do once she's given birth?" I ask.

Kain shrugs. "We get her to hospital like Brook said. After that, she isn't our problem."

"She should be in the ground for what she's done."

"Yeah, she should be, but she's a new mum. It's not the sort of kill I want on my conscience."

Another scream rings out followed by a baby crying. "Thank fuck for that," I mutter. I'm itching to get Brook alone so I can explain everything and see if there'll ever be a chance of us now the truth is out.

"Maybe we should stay here tonight. It's late, and we can get Cooper to bring the truck tomorrow and get Melissa to the hospital." I nod in agreement, since we can't take the baby on our motorbikes. "How's it feel to be near Brook again, man?"

I smile. "Like I can breathe again."

"Do you think you two will sort shit out?"

"Who knows. We've been through a lot, and I don't even know if those fuckers hurt her. There's a lot to talk about, but I want her back," I say. "Doesn't mean she's gonna want me, does it? I've put her through a lot."

"Brother, it wasn't your fault. Brook will see that, she loves you."

The door opens and Brook steps out. "You okay, darlin'?" Kain asks her, and she nods.

"Melissa's doing good. It's a boy." Brook lowers herself to sit down next to me. "It's silly, but I can't help feeling sad. That might never be me." A stray tear runs down her cheek and she swipes at it. "It's stupid to be jealous over Melissa. It was emotional in there, even though I hate her."

"We don't owe her anything, Brook. After everything she's done, she's lucky I've not sent her to join her dad and Hawk." I feel bitter and I'm not sure that will ever go away, but seeing Brook like this pisses me off some more. She deserves to have a kid, Melissa doesn't.

"I'm just being silly. High emotions and all that." She shrugs, adding a smile.

"It's not silly, Brook. You've had a real shitty time. If we could change things . . ." Kain sighs. "Well, we let you down, the whole club did, and I feel bad about that. You're one of us, you've always been one of us, and I know you have a life now, a different one to what you had with us, but we miss you. And if you wanna come back, if you can ever forgive us, we'd always welcome you back." Kain lights a cigarette. "I'll give you two a minute alone."

I wait for him to disappear into the trees before sighing heavily. It's been a crazy few months, and now we're here with no barriers between us, I don't know where to start. I've never been one for talking, Brook knows that, and she takes my hand. "How are you feeling?" she asks. Trust her to worry about me instead of herself.

"Baby, I don't even know where to begin. I've spent months feeing guilt for something that never happened, and now, I feel guilty because you've been put through all of this."

"It was all out of our control, Tann. We got played."

"So, now what?" I ask. Her beautiful face looks tired, and I want to take her home and snuggle her into my side. I miss holding her.

"I'm not sure. Melissa said something that kind of made me think. She said that it was easy to come between us." I don't like the look that passes over her face, and I sit up straight, tugging at my beard nervously. "And she was right. She came right in there and stuck herself between us, and we let that happen. Maybe we weren't as solid as we thought."

"What are you saying?"

"I'm saying we can't just go back to being us, Tanner. Things have changed . . . we've changed."

Emotions begin to stir, and I suddenly have the urge to move. I stand abruptly, and Brook follows me with her sad eyes. "You're wrong," I mutter, jumping down the steps and turning to face her. "We were solid. That kind of shit would have torn anyone apart. I can't handle it if you're telling me never, Brook. I just can't." I head after Kain, hoping a walk will clear my head.

CHAPTER FOURTEEN

Brook

I watch Tanner disappear into the trees, and my heart squeezes. I've spent months praying that I was living a nightmare and I'd wake up to find it was nothing more than a bad dream. I love Tanner, there's no doubt about it, but Melissa's right. She just walked right into our relationship and crushed it. I never doubted her lie—I accepted what she told me and just left. If our love was so strong, wouldn't I have questioned it? Wouldn't I have had faith in my man . . . in our love for one another?

The door opens and Melissa steps out. She looks pale and tired. "Are you okay?" I ask.

"I'm really sorry," she utters. She lifts her arms and points a gun at me. "If you try and stop me, I'm gonna kill you."

"What the fuck? What are you talking about?"

She crouches down, picking Tanner's bag up from by the door. "I'm gonna leave. Stay right there, and don't make me use this gun." I follow her with my eyes as she backs down the steps.

"Hold on, what about the baby?" Melissa begins to cry, her hand shakes uncontrollably. "Mel, listen, you've just had a baby, you aren't thinking straight. We need to get you checked over. If you want to leave after that, then I won't stop you, but at least let me get you to a hospital. Cooper's bringing the truck. I can get him here sooner if you'd like?"

"I can't," she sobs. "I just can't. I'm so sorry . . . for everything." She climbs onto Kain's motorcycle, wincing in pain but lowering the gun as she kicks it to life.

My mouth falls open in shock. "You can't just leave, you're supposed to rest, you must be tired and sore?"

"I have no choice," she replies and then she speeds off. I have no mobile to call Tanner back, so I look around, unsure of what to do next, and then crying from inside the cabin reminds me that Melissa's left without her newborn son.

I slowly walk into the cabin. The bundle is wriggling in the centre of the bed, and I hesitate as I peer at the screaming little boy. "Erm, hey, little man," I whisper cautiously. He cries harder. "Shit," I mutter. I scoop the baby into my arms, and he instantly settles. He's still naked, wrapped loosely in a cotton sheet. I turn to the door at the sound of heavy footsteps approaching, and Tanner stops the minute he spots me with the baby.

"We heard the motorbike," he says, confusion on his face.

"She went . . . she took your bag and Kain's bike."

"Arr, man," yells Kain from outside, "Where the fuck's my motorbike?"

"Shit, she left without the kid," mutters Tanner as Kain appears behind him.

"Tell me that bitch didn't take my motorbike," he groans.

"Your bike is the least of our problems. She's taken the money and left the kid," growls Tanner.

I stare down into the sweet face of the baby. His lips are pouted, and his eyes are closed. "We need to get Cooper to come get us now. This little one will need feeding soon. I'm not sure if Melissa fed him when I left her alone in here."

Kain pulls out his phone. "I'm on it," he says.

Tanner steps towards me, looking into the sheet that covers the baby bundle. "It suits you," he murmurs. "You look sexy as hell barefoot and holding a baby."

"I can't believe she just left him like that. How can she do that?" I feel tears roll down my cheeks, and Tanner uses his thumbs to wipe them away.

"Yah know, there's an easy fix here. He's got no parents, and you want a kid so badly . . ." He leaves the statement hanging in the air.

I gasp. "No, I can't just take someone else's baby, Tanner."

"Nobody knows, and you'd make a great mum."

"But he isn't mine to take. I can't do that."

Tanner shrugs. "It was just a suggestion, but the thought of him growing up in foster care . . ."

I gently stroke the baby's head. There are thousands of people out there wanting to adopt babies, so this little one wouldn't go into the system for long. Someone would take him in.

Mila places a steaming coffee down before me. Cooper had set off straight away to get us, and now, we're all back at the clubhouse, staring down at Melissa's baby as he sucks hard on a bottle of milk. The good thing about the club is there're always mums around, so sorting out a newborn is no issue.

Clothes, a cot, and nappies were on hand before I'd even arrived.

"So, now what?" she asks, stroking a finger over the baby's head. "He's such a cutie."

I shrug. "No idea."

"Have you thought about what this could mean?" she asks warily. "It's like it was meant to be."

I sigh. "Don't you start. I've already had Tanner saying the same. I can't just keep a baby because I want it."

"He's been abandoned. Besides, she took a load of cash from Tanner."

"So, selling and buying babies is suddenly legal, is it?" I snap.

Mila places her hand over mine and smiles reassuringly. "Sweetie, all I'm saying is that she told Tanner this kid was his, right? If we didn't know it wasn't, then legally, Tanner would have a right. We wouldn't even be having this discussion, would we?"

I think over what she's saying, and nod, guessing she's right. "But I know the truth, Mila. I'm not sure I can live such a huge lie."

"Just for once, Brook, can't you take what you want? You want a baby so badly, and after everything Melissa did, you deserve happiness. This could be it, your ticket."

"It feels wrong. How would I register him?"

"Cooper will sort all that. You don't have to worry. Just think it over."

Tanner approaches. "You want me to take him while you drink your coffee?" he asks. He hasn't held the baby at all, and I smile gratefully, letting him lift him from my arms.

He looks mighty fine holding the baby, and Mila nudges me. "Jeez, after seeing how sexy that whole image is, you can't give the baby back." I laugh. Maybe Mila is right. I can give this baby such a great life, and I'll never get this opportunity again.

"Did they touch you?" asks Mila, looking down at her hands.

"No. Kenny almost did, but Tanner saved the day by distracting him with money. Other than that, the worst I had to do was sleep on the ground."

"I can see bruises," she adds.

"Club life," I say, adding a grin.

"Does that mean you still want to be part of the club life?"

"I missed it so bad. Living in the apartment was lonely compared to being here. I missed the kids running around and the guys being arseholes. Kain said I should come back, but isn't it awkward after everything?" It's been playing on my mind since Kain suggested it. Coming back like nothing's happened is strange.

"Seriously, after everything in the history of this club, you coming back is the least awkward thing to happen." I laugh because she's right. Cooper's dead ex returning was definitely way worse than my situation.

"Why don't I get a prospect to set up a cot in the spare room? Get a good sleep, spend some time with the little one, and then make all the important decisions," she suggests, and I nod. Sleep sounds amazing right now.

I lay the baby in the cot, and he didn't even stir. After guzzling down his milk, he seems happy enough. As I climb into bed, my thoughts turn to Melissa and how she must be feeling right now. If I decide to stay here, at least if she ever comes back, she'll know where to find her baby. If I gave him to the state, she'd never be able to find him, and how would I even begin to explain to social services what's happened tonight? I drift off with thoughts of me and Tanner raising someone else's baby. I like the idea of being with Tanner again, and I go to sleep smiling.

At some point, I turn and hit something hard. I open one eye and Tanner is sitting next to me holding the baby. "Hey, sleepy," he whispers. "The little thing cried, so I stuffed a bottle in his mouth, and he's not made a sound since," he adds, smiling down at the bundle in his arms. I push myself to sit and peer at the sleeping baby.

"And there I was thinking you never wanted kids."

"Yeah, well, I feel bad for this little guy. No parents and he's only a few hours old."

I stroke the baby's tiny hand. "Yeah, it's a pretty shitty start," I whisper. Tanner kisses me on the head, and I lay against his huge bicep. "Mila thinks we should keep him."

"You said we," notes Tanner, and I smile, kissing his arm.

"It won't be easy. We have a lot to work through. I want to know it all, Tann, everything that happened with you and Kenny when you were a kid." He tries to protest, but I sit up straight and stare him down. "I know you say it's in the past, that you don't need to tell me because it isn't important, but it is. It's what makes you, you, and I want to know it all. We need to be stronger this time. I want more than just fucking and arguing. I was in the dark on it all, and maybe had I of known, I might have been wary of Melissa. I might have questioned her."

Tanner places a hand against my cheek and nods reluctantly. "Okay, I'll try."

"I want date nights at least once a week," I add, and he groans. He hates all that romantic stuff, but if I'm gonna agree to come back to him, he needs to show me that he's just as serious about us working.

I raise my eyebrow and he relents. "Fine."

"And no more fucking me into getting your own way. You must start listening to me instead of steamrolling me when you don't like what I'm saying."

He sighs. "Shit, mama, you're taking full advantage of this."

"And we stay here. If Melissa comes back for her baby, she'll come here. We'll raise this baby as a club kid, but if his mum comes back, we'll have to say goodbye."

"No," he huffs. "No way. You know how hard that will be on us. What if she doesn't come back until he's ten? That's ten years of us loving him. Cooper knows someone who can fake a birth certificate. We can put me down as the father and then he'll be ours."

I shake my head. It would be easy to do that, and my heart begs me to agree, but it wouldn't be fair to this baby or Melissa. I know she isn't a good person, and maybe if we don't hear anything for the next few years, we can look into making him ours, but for now, she needs time to think about her decision. I'm happy to look after her boy while she does that. "You'll need a birth certificate, and you'll have to say you're the father in case he needs medical care, but as for us keeping him as our own, for now, that isn't a possibility. Melissa may wake up tomorrow and realise she made a mistake."

Tanner looks down at the bundle. "Fine, whatever you want, Brook. I just want us back. I want to wake up and know you're here with me again."

I take his hand in mine. "I love you, Tanner." It feels good to say it again. I kiss him gently. "I missed you so much."

"You have no idea," he groans, and I grin at his obvious erection.

"Oh baby," I mutter, "you'd better go find us a babysitter."

Tanner scrambles from the bed with the baby in his arms. "I'll be back. Don't move," he orders, rushing from the room.

Six months later...

Tanner

Renewing our wedding vows was my idea, and watching Brook across the room right now makes my heart swell with pride. She looks amazing in the short, white lace dress, with Caleb in her arms. We've settled into parenthood like pros. Brook was born to be a mother and she's doing so amazing. We haven't heard from Melissa, but I have a guy on her, watching. I needed to know if she's ever gonna come back for this kid, because honestly, I don't know if I can give him up now. The day will come where I'll have to make a hard decision, either force her to sign parental consent over to us or send her to ground to join Hawk and her dad. This is club life, and I won't give up what I don't want to, not again.

Brook smiles at me from across the room, giving me a little wave. My mum's showing her photographs of when I was a kid. We didn't tell her that Caleb isn't mine biologically, and so she insists that he looks exactly like I did at that age.

I make my way over to them. "Ma, put those away." I sigh, wrapping my arm around Brook. She looks up at me, smiling fondly, and I plant a kiss on her lips. "About time we made a toast, don't yah think?" I whistle to get everyone's attention and the room quietens down.

"I just want to thank you all for joining us today. Renewing our vows was the best idea I ever had, and having you all here means so much." A few of the guys cheer. "But we have some other news." I pause for dramatic affect and a few of the ol' ladies complain, telling me to get the hell on with it. "Most of you know we've been trying for a baby, and with the help of the medical professionals, we had it confirmed this morning that we're expecting." The room erupts into cheers and congratulations. Kissing Brook and then Caleb, I feel like the proudest man in the world. My perfect growing family. I got a second chance to be with the only person I've ever loved and nothing's gonna come between us again. I'll make sure of it.

A note from me to you

Oh my, where do I start? When I wrote the first book in the Splintered Heart Series, it was supposed to be a standalone. A few readers got in touch and asked for Kain and Harper's story, so I gave it a go. After that, I had so many requests for Tanner and Brook to have their own story. I can't lie, it didn't speak to me for a while, and I must have picked up my laptop a thousand times before finally writing it. This ended up being my most favourite one in the series! Once I began writing, it flowed so naturally. I had no outline, not much past history, and no idea where it was going, yet it came together beautifully.

Thank you to everyone who pushed for this story. I hope you love it! Please share a review or rating on whichever platform you download, it helps authors like me, out.

I'm a UK author, based in Nottinghamshire. I live with my husband of many years, our two teenage boys and our four little dogs. I write MC and Mafia romance with plenty of drama and chaos. I also love to read similar books. Before I became a full-time author, I was a teaching assistant working in a primary school.

If you'd like to follow my writing journey, join my readers group on Facebook, the link is below. You can also use that link if you're a book blogger, I'd love you to sign up to my team.

For all things Nicola Jane, head here...https://linktr.ee/NicolaJaneUK

Popular books by Nicola Jane

The Kings Reapers MC
Riggs' Ruin https://mybook.to/RiggsRuin
Capturing Cree https://mybook.to/CapturingCree
Wrapped in Chains https://mybook.to/WrappedinChains
Saving Blu https://mybook.to/SavingBlu
Riggs' Saviour https://mybook.to/RiggsSaviour
Taming Blade https://mybook.to/TamingBlade
Misleading Lake https://mybook.to/MisleadingLake
Surviving Storm https://mybook.to/SurvivingStorm
Ravens Place https://mybook.to/RavensPlace

Playing Vinn https://mybook.to/PlayingVinn

The Perished Riders MC
Maverick https://mybook.to/Maverick-Perished
Scar https://mybook.to/Scar-Perished
Grim https://mybook.to/Grim-Perished
Ghost https://mybook.to/GhostBk4
Dice https://mybook.to/DiceBk5

The Hammers MC (Splintered Hearts Series)
Cooper https://mybook.to/CooperSHS
Kain https://mybook.to/Kain
Tanner https://mybook.to/TannerSH

Printed in Great Britain
by Amazon